BRING THE JUBILEE

Ward Moore

The right of Ward Moore to be identified as the author
of this work has been asserted by him in accordance with
the Copyright, Designs and Patents Act 1988.

This edition published in Great Britain in 2001 by

Gollancz
An imprint of the Orion Publishing Group
Orion House, 5 Upper St Martin's Lane, London WC2H 9EA

5 7 9 10 8 6

A CIP catalogue record for this book is available
from the British Library

ISBN 978-1-85798-764-5

Printed in Great Britain by
Clays Ltd, St Ives plc

www.orionbooks.co.uk

For Tony Boucher and Mick McComas
who liked this story

What he will he does, and does so much
That proof is call'd impossibility
TROILUS AND CRESSIDA

It is always the puzzle of the nature of time that brings our thoughts to a standstill. And if time is so fundamental that an understanding of its true nature is for ever beyond our reach, then so also in all probability is a decision in the age-long controversy between determination and free will.

The Mysterious Universe by JAMES JEANS

Contents

1. LIFE IN THE TWENTY-SIX STATES

*A*LTHOUGH I am writing this in the year 1877, I was not born until 1921. Neither the dates nor the tenses are error—let me explain:

I was born, as I say, in 1921, but it was not until the early 1930's, when I was about ten, that I began to understand what a peculiarly frustrate and disinherited world was about me. Perhaps my approach to realization was through the crayon portrait of Granpa Hodgins which hung, very solemnly, over the mantel.

Granpa Hodgins after whom I was named, perhaps a little grandiloquently, Hodgins McCormick Backmaker, had been a veteran of the War of Southron Independence. Like so many young men he had put on a shapeless blue uniform in response to the call of the ill-advised and headstrong—or martyred—Mr Lincoln. Depending on which of my lives' viewpoints you take.

Granpa lost an arm on the Great Retreat to Philadelphia after the fall of Washington to General Lee's victorious Army of Northern Virginia, so his war ended some six months before the capitulation at Reading and the acknowledgment of the independence of the Confederate States on July 4, 1864. One-armed and embittered, Granpa came home to Wappinger Falls and, like his fellow veterans, tried to remake his life in a different and increasingly hopeless world.

On its face the Peace of Richmond was a just and even generous disposition of a defeated foe by the victor. (Both sides—for different reasons—remembered the mutiny of

1

the Unreconstructed Federals in the Armies of the Cumberland and the Tennessee who, despite defeat at Chattanooga, could not forget Vicksburg or Port Hudson and fought bloodily against the order to surrender.) The South could easily have carved the country up to suit its most fiery patriots, even to the point of detaching the West and making a protectorate of it. Instead the chivalrous Southrons contented themselves with drawing the new boundary along traditional lines. The Mason-Dixon gave them Delaware and Maryland, but they generously returned the panhandle of western Virginia jutting above it. Missouri was naturally included in the Confederacy, but of the disputed territory Colorado and Deseret were conceded to the old Union; only Kansas and California as well as—for obvious defensive reasons—Nevada's tip went to the South.

But the Peace of Richmond had also laid the cost of the war on the beaten North and this was what crippled Granpa Hodgins more than the loss of his arm. The postwar inflation entered the galloping stage during the Vallandigham Administration, became dizzying in the time of President Seymour and precipitated the food riots of 1873 and '74. It was only after the election of President Butler by the Whigs in 1876 and the reorganization and drastic deflation following that money and property became stable, but by this time all normal values were destroyed. Meanwhile the indemnities had to be paid regularly in gold. Granpa and hundreds of thousands like him just never seemed to get back on their feet.

How well I remember, as a small boy in the 1920's and '30s, my mother and father talking bitterly of how the War had ruined everything. They were not speaking of the then fairly recent Emperors' War of 1914-16, but of the War of Southron Independence which still, nearly seventy years later, blighted what was left of the United States.

Nor were they unique or peculiar in this. Men who slouched in the smithy while Father shod their horses, or gathered every month around the postoffice waiting for the notice of the winning lottery numbers to be put up, as often cursed the Confederates or discussed what might have been if Meade had been a better general or Lee a worse one, as they did the new-type bicycles with clockwork auxiliaries to make pedaling uphill easier, or the latest scandal about the French Emperor, Napoleon VI.

I tried to imagine what it must have been like in Granpa Hodgins' day, to visualize the lost past—that strange bright era when, if it could be believed, folk like ourselves and our neighbors had owned their farms outright and didnt pay rent to the bank or give half the crop to a landlord. I searched the wiggling crayon lines that composed Granpa Hodgins' face for some sign that set him apart from his descendants.

"But what did he *do* to lose the farm?" I used to ask my mother.

"Do? Didnt do anything. Couldnt help himself. Go along now and do your chores; Ive a terrible batch of work to get out."

How could Granpa's not doing anything result so disastrously? I could not understand this any more than I could the bygone time when a man could nearly always get a job for wages which would support himself and a family, before the system of indenture became so common that practically the only alternative to pauperism was to sell oneself to a company.

Indenting I understood all right, for there was a mill in Wappinger Falls which wove a shoddy cloth very different from the goods my mother produced on her handloom. Mother, even in her late forties, could have indented there for a good price, and she admitted that the work would be easier than weaving homespun to compete with their product. But, as she used to say with an obstinate shake of her head, "Free I was born and free I'll die."

In Granpa Hodgins' day, if one could believe the folktales or family legends, men and women married young and had large families; there might have been five generations between him and me instead of two. And many uncles, aunts, cousins, brothers and sisters. Now late marriages and only children were the rule.

If it hadnt been for the War— This was the basic theme stated with variations suited to the particular circumstance. If it hadnt been for the War the most energetic young men and women would not turn to emigration; visiting foreigners would not come as to a slum; and the great powers would think twice before sending troops to restore order every time one of their citizens was molested. If it hadnt been for the War the detestable buyer from Boston—detestable to my mother, but rather fascinating to me with his brightly colored vest and smell of soap and hair tonic—would not have come regularly to offer her a miserable price for her weaving.

"Foreigner!" she would always exclaim after he left; "sending good cloth out of the country."

Once my father ventured, "He's only doing what he's paid for."

"Trust a Backmaker to stand up for foreigners. Like father, like son; suppose you'd let the whole thieving crew in if you had your way."

So was first hinted the scandal of Grandfather Backmaker. No enlarged portrait of him hung anywhere, much less over the mantel. I got the impression my father's father had been not only a foreigner by birth, but a shady character in his own right, a man who kept on believing in the things for which Granpa Hodgins fought after they were proved wrong. I don't know how I learned that Grandfather Backmaker had made speeches advocating equal rights for Negroes or protesting the mass lynchings so popular in the North, in contrast to the humane treatment accorded these non-citizens in the Confederacy. Nor do I remember where I heard he had been run out of several places before finally settling in Wappinger Falls or that all his life people had muttered darkly at his back, "Dirty Abolitionist!"—a very deep imprecation indeed. I only know that as a consequence of this taint my father, a meek, hardworking, worried little man, was completely dominated by my mother who never let him forget that a Hodgins or a McCormick was worth dozens of Backmakers.

I must have been a sore trial to her for I showed no sign of proper Hodgins gumption, such as she displayed herself and which surely kept us all—though precariously —free. For one thing I was remarkably unhandy and awkward, of little use in the hundred necessary chores around our dilapidated house. I could not pick up a hammer at her command to do something about fixing the loose weatherboards on the east side without mashing my thumb or splitting the aged, unpainted wood. I could not hoe the kitchen garden without damaging precious vegetables and leaving weeds intact. I could shovel snow in the winter at a tremendous rate for I was strong and had endurance, but work requiring manual dexterity baffled me. I fumbled in harnessing Bessie, our mare, or hitching her to the cart for my father's trips to Poughkeepsie, and as for helping him on the farm or in his smithy I'm afraid my efforts drove that mild man nearest to a temper he ever came. He would lay the reins on the plowhorse's back or his hammer down on the anvil and say mournfully:

"Better see if you can help your mother, Hodge. Youre only in my way here."

On only one score did I come near pleasing Mother: I learned to read and write early, and exhibited some proficiency. But even here there was a flaw; she looked upon literacy as something which distinguished Hodginses and McCormicks from the ruck who had to make their mark, as an accomplishment which might somehow and unspecifiedly lead away from poverty. I found reading an end in itself, which probably reminded her of my father's laxity or Grandfather Backmaker's subversion.

"Make something of yourself, Hodge," she admonished me often. "You can't change the world"—an obvious allusion to Grandfather Backmaker—"but you can do something with it as it is if you try hard enough. There's always some way out."

Yet she did not approve of the postoffice lottery, on which so many pinned their hopes of escape from poverty or indenture. In this she and my father were agreed; both believed in hard work rather than chance.

Still, chance could help even the steadiest toiler. I remember the time a minibile—one of the small, trackless locomotives—broke down not a quarter of a mile from Father's smithy. This was a golden, unparalleled, unbelievable opportunity. Minibiles, like any other luxury, were rare in the United States though they were common enough in prosperous countries like the German Union or the Confederacy. We had to rely for our transportation on the never-failing horse or on the railroads, wornout and broken down as they were. For decades the great issue in Congress was the never completed Pacific transcontinental line, though British America had one and the Confederate States seven. (Sailing balloons, economical and fairly common, were still looked upon with some suspicion.) Only a rare millionaire with connections in Frankfurt, Washington-Baltimore or Leesburg could afford to indulge in a costly and complicated minibile requiring a trained driver to bounce it over the rutted and chuckholed roads. Only an extraordinarily adventurous spirit would leave the tar-surfaced streets of New York or its sister city of Brooklyn, where the minibiles' solid rubber tires could at worst find traction on the horse or cable-car rails, for the morasses or washboard roads which were the only highways north of the Harlem River.

When one did, the jolting, jouncing and shaking inevitably broke or disconnected one of the delicate parts in its complex mechanism. Then the only recourse—apart from telegraphing back to the city if the traveler broke down near an instrument—was to the closest blacksmith. Smiths rarely knew much of the principles of the minibiles, but with the broken part before them they could fabricate a passable duplicate and, unless the machine had suffered severe damage, put it back in place. It was customary for such a craftsman to compensate himself for the time taken away from horseshoeing or spring-fitting—or just absently chewing on an oatstraw—by demanding exorbitant remuneration, amounting to perhaps twenty-five or thirty cents an hour, thus avenging his rural poverty and self-sufficiency upon the effete wealth and helplessness of the urban excursionist.

Such a golden opportunity befell my father, as I said, during the fall of 1933, when I was twelve. The driver had made his way to the smithy, leaving the owner of the minibile marooned and fuming in the enclosed passenger seat. A hasty visit convinced Father, who could repair a clock or broken rake with equal dexterity, that his only course was to bring the machine to the forge where he could heat and straighten a part not easy to disassemble. (The driver, the owner, and Father all repeated the name of the part often enough, but so inept have I been with "practical" things all my life that I couldnt recall it ten minutes, much less thirty years later.)

"Hodge, run and get the mare and ride over to Jones's. Don't try to saddle her—go bareback. Ask Mr Jones to kindly lend me his team."

"I'll give the boy a quarter dollar for himself if he's back with the team in twenty minutes," added the owner of the minibile, sticking his head out of the window.

I won't say I was off like the wind, for my life's work has given me a distaste for exaggeration or hyperbole, but I moved faster than I ever had before. A quarter, a whole shining silver quarter, a day's full wage for the boy who could find odd jobs, half the day's pay of a grown man who wasnt indented or worked extra hours—all for myself, to spend as I wished!

I ran all the way back to the barn, led Bessie out by her halter and jumped on her broad back, my enthralling daydream growing and deepening each moment. With my quarter safely got I could perhaps persuade my father to take me along on his next trip to Poughkeepsie; in the shops there I could find some yards of figured cotton for Mother, or a box of cigars to which Father was partial but rarely bought for himself, or an unimagined something for Mary McCutcheon, some three years older than I, with whom it had so recently become disturbing as well as imperative to wrestle—in secret of course so as not to show oneself unmanly in sporting with a weak girl instead of another boy.

It never even occurred to me, as it would have to most, to invest in an eighth of a lottery ticket. Not only were my parents sternly against this popular gamble, but I myself felt a strangely puritanical aversion to meddling with my fortune.

Or I could take the entire quarter into Newman's Book and Clock Store. Here I could not afford one of the latest

English or Confederate books—even the novels I disdained cost fifty cents in their original and thirty in the pirated United States' edition—but what treasures there were in the twelve-and-a-half cent reprints and the dime classics!

With Bessie's legs moving steadily beneath me I pored over in my imagination Mr Newman's entire stock, which I knew by heart from examinations lulled by the steady ticking of his other, and no doubt more salable, merchandise. My quarter would buy two reprints, but I would read them in as many evenings and be no better off than before until their memory faded and I could read them again. Better to invest in paperbacked adventure stories giving sharp, breathless pictures of life in the West or rekindling the glories of the War. True, they were written almost entirely by Confederate authors and I was, perhaps thanks to Granpa Hodgins and my mother, a devout partisan of the lost cause of Sheridan and Sherman and Thomas. But patriotism couldnt steel me against the excitement of the Confederate paperbacks; literature simply ignored the boundary stretching to the Pacific.

I had finally determined to invest all my twenty-five cents, not in five paperbound volumes but in ten of the same in secondhand or shopworn condition, when I suddenly realized that I had been riding Bessie for some considerable time. I looked around, rather dazed by the abrupt translation from the dark and slightly musty interior of Newman's store to the bright countryside, to find with dismay that Bessie hadnt taken me to the Jones farm after all but on some private tour of her own in the opposite direction.

I'm afraid this little anecdote is pointless—it was momentarily pointed enough for me that evening, for in addition to the loss of the promised quarter I received a thorough whacking with a willow switch from my mother after my father had, as usual, dolefully refused his parental duty—except perhaps that it shows how in pursuing the dream I could lose the reality.

My feeling that books were a part of life, and the most important part, was no passing phase. Other boys in their early teens dreamed of going to the wilds of Dakotah,

Montana or Wyoming, indenting to a company run by a young and beautiful woman—this was also a favorite paperback theme—discovering the loot hidden by a gang, or emigrating to Australia or the South African Republic. Or else they faced the reality of indenture, carrying on the family farm, or petty trade. I only wanted to be allowed to read.

I knew this ambition, if that is the proper word, to be outrageous and unheard of. It was also practically impossible. The school at Wappinger Falls, a survival from the days of compulsory attendance and an object of doubt in the eyes of the taxpayers, taught as little as possible as quickly as possible. Parents needed the help of their children to survive or to build up a small reserve in the illusory hope of buying free of indenture. Both my mother and my teachers looked askance at my longing to persist past an age when my contemporaries were making themselves economically useful.

Nor, even supposing I had the fees, could the shabby, fusty Academy at Poughkeepsie—originally designed for the education of the well-to-do—provide what I wanted. Not that I was clear at all as to just what this was; I only knew that commercial arithmetic, surveying, or any of the other subjects taught there, were not the answer to my desires.

There was certainly no money for any college. Our position had grown slowly worse; my father talked of selling the smithy and indenting. My dreams of Harvard or Yale were as idle as Father's of making a good crop and getting out of debt. Nor did I know then, as I was to find out later, that the colleges were increasingly provincialized and decayed, contrasting painfully with the flourishing universities of the Confederacy and Europe. The average man asked what the United States needed colleges for anyway; those who attended them only learned discontent and to question time-honored institutions. Constant scrutiny of the faculties, summary firing of all instructors suspected of abnormal ideas, did not seem to improve the situation or raise the standards of teaching.

My mother, now that I was getting beyond the switching

age, lectured me firmly and at length on idleness and self-indulgence. "It's a hard world, Hodge, and no one's going to give you anything you don't earn. Your father's an easy-going man; too easy-going for his own good, but he always knows where his duty lies."

"Yes, maam," I responded politely, not quite seeing what she was driving at.

"Hard, honest work—that's the only thing. Not hoping or wishing or thinking miracles will happen to you. Work hard and keep yourself free. Don't depend on circumstances or other people, and don't blame them for your own shortcomings. Be your own man. That's the only way you'll ever be where you want to."

She spoke of responsibility and duty as though they were measurable quantities, but the gentler parts of such equations, the factors of affection and pity, were never mentioned. I don't want to give the impression that ours was a particularly puritanical family; I know our neighbors had of necessity much the same grim outlook. But I felt guiltily vulnerable, not merely on the score of wanting more schooling, but because of something else which would have shocked my mother beyond forgiveness.

My early tussles with Mary McCutcheon had the natural consequences, but she had found me a too-youthful partner and had taken her interests elsewhere. For my part I now turned to Agnes Jones, a suddenly alluring young woman grown from the skinny kid I'd always brushed away. Agnes sympathized with my aspirations and encouraged me most pleasantly. However her specific plans for my future were limited to marrying her and helping her father on his farm, which seemed no great advance over what I could look forward to at home.

And there I was certainly no asset; I ate three hearty meals a day and occupied a bed. I was conscious of the looks and smiles which followed me. A great lout of seventeen, too lazy to do a stroke of work, always wandering around with his head in the clouds or lying with his nose stuck in a book. Too bad; and the Backmakers such industrious folks too. I could feel what the shock of my behavior with Agnes added to my idleness would be to my mother.

Yet I was neither depraved nor very different from the other youths of Wappinger Falls, who not only took their pleasures where they found them, but often more forcibly than persuasively. I did not analyze it fully or clearly, but I was at least to some extent aware of the essentially loveless atmosphere around me. The rigid convention of late marriages bred an exaggerated respect for chastity which had two sides: sisters' and daughters' honor was sternly avenged with no protest from society, and undiscovered seduction produced that much more gratification. But both retribution and venery were somewhat mechanical; they were the expected rather than the inescapable passions. Revivalists—and we country people had a vast fondness for those itinerants who came periodically to castigate us for our sins—denounced our laxity and pointed to the virtues of our grandparents and greatgrandparents. We accepted their advice with such modifications as suited us, which was not at all what they intended.

And this was how I took my mother's admonition to be my own man. What debts I owed her and my father seemed best discharged by relieving them of the burden of my keep, since I was clearly not fitting myself to reverse the balance. The notion that there was an emotional obligation on either side hardly occurred to me; I doubt if it did to them. Toward Agnes Jones I felt no debt at all.

A few months after my seventeenth birthday I packed my three most cherished books in my good white cotton shirt, and having bade a most romantic goodbye to Agnes, one which would certainly have consummated her hopes had her father come upon us, I left Wappinger Falls and set out for New York.

2. OF DECISIONS, MINIBILES, AND TINUGRAPHS

I THOUGHT I could do the walk of some eighty miles in four days, allowing time to swap work for food, supposing I found farmers or housewives agreeable to the exchange. June made it no hardship to sleep outdoors, and the old post road ran close enough to the Hudson for any bathing I might want to do.

The dangers of the trip were part of the pattern of life in the United States in 1938. I didnt particularly fear being robbed by a roving gang for I was sure organized predators would disdain so obviously unprofitable a prey, and individual thieves I felt I could take care of, but I was not anxious to be picked up as a vagrant by any of the three police forces, national, state, or local. As a freeman I was more exposed to this chance than an indent would be, with a work-card on his person and a company behind him. A freeman was fair game for the constables, state troopers, or revenuers to recruit, after a perfunctory trial, into one of the chain gangs upon whom the roads, canals and other public works were dependent.

Some wondered why the roads were so bad in spite of all this apparent surplus of labor and were dubious of the explanation that surfacing was expensive and it was impossible to maintain unsurfaced highways in good condition. Only the hint that prisoners had been seen working around the estates of the great Whig families or had been lent to some enterprise operated by foreign capital brought knowing nods.

At seventeen possible disasters are not brooded over.

I resolved to be wary, and then dismissed thoughts of police, gangs and all unpleasantness. The future was mine to make as my mother had insisted, and I was taking the first steps in shaping it.

I started off briskly, passing at first through villages long familiar; then, getting beyond the territory I had known all my life, I slowed down often enough to gaze at something new and strange, or to wander into wood or pasture for wild strawberries or early blueberries. I covered less ground than I had intended by the time I found a farmhouse, after inquiring at several others, where the woman was willing to give me supper and even let me sleep in the barn in return for splitting a sizable stack of logs into kindling and milking two cows.

Exercise and hot food must have counteracted the excitement of the day, for I fell asleep immediately and didnt waken till quite a while after sunup. It was another warm, fine morning; soon the post road led, not between shabby villages and towns or struggling farms, but past the stone or brick walls of opulent estates. Now and then I caught a glimpse between old, well-tended trees of magnificent houses either a century old or built to resemble those dating from that prosperous time. I could not but share the general dislike for the wealthy Whigs who owned these places, their riches contrasting with the common poverty and deriving from exploitation of the United States as a colony, but I could not help enjoying the beauty of their surroundings.

The highway was better traveled here also; I passed other walkers, quite a few wagons, a carriage or two, several peddlers and a number of ladies and gentlemen on horseback. This was the first time I'd seen women riding astride, a practice shocking to the sensitivities of Wappinger Falls which also condemned the fashion, imported from the Chinese Empire by way of England, of feminine trousers. Having learned that women were bipedal, both customs seemed sensible to me.

I had the post road to myself for some miles between turns when I heard a commotion beyond the stone wall to my left. This was followed by an angry shout and shrill words impossible to distinguish. My progress halted, I instinctively shifted my bundle to my left hand as though to leave my right free for defence, but against what I had no idea.

The shouts came closer; a boy of about my own age scrambled frantically over the wall, dislodging some of the smaller lichen-covered rocks on top and sending them rolling into the ditch. He looked at me, startled, then paused for a long instant at the road's edge, undecided which way to run.

He was barefoot and wore a jute sack as a shirt, with holes cut for his arms, and ragged cotton pants. His face was little browner than my own had often been at the end of a summer's work under a burning sun.

He came to the end of indecision and started across the highway, legs pumping high, head turned watchfully. A splendid tawny stallion cleared the wall in a soaring jump, his rider bellowing, "There you are, you damned black coon!"

He rode straight for the fugitive, quirt upraised, lips thickened and eyes rolling in rage. The victim dodged and turned; in no more doubt than I that the horseman meant to ride him down. He darted by me, so close I heard the labored rasp of breathing.

The rider swerved, and he too twisted around me as though I were the post at the far turn of a racecourse. Reflexively I put out my hand to grab at the reins and stop the assault. Indeed, my fingers actually touched the leather and grasped it for a fraction of a second before they fell away.

Then I was alone in the road again as both pursued and pursuer vaulted back over the fence. The whole scene of anger and terror could not have lasted two minutes; I strained my ears to hear the shouts coming from farther and farther away. Quiet fell again; a squirrel flirted his tail and sped down one tree trunk and up another. The episode might never have happened.

I shifted my bundle back and began walking again—less briskly now. My legs felt heavy and there was an involuntary twitch in the muscles of my arm.

Why hadnt I held on to the rein and delayed the hunter, at least long enough to give his quarry a fair start? What had made me draw back? It had not been fear, at least in the usual sense, for I knew I wasnt timorous of the horseman. I was sure I could have dragged him down if he had taken his quirt to me.

Yet I had been afraid. Afraid of interfering, of meddling in affairs which were no concern of mine, of risking action on quick judgment. I had been immobilized by the fear of asserting my sympathies, my presumptions, against events.

Walking slowly down the road I experienced deep shame. I might, I could have saved someone from hurt; I had perhaps had the power for a brief instant to change the course of a whole life. I had been guilty of a cowardice far worse than mere fear for my skin. I could have wept with mortification—done anything, in fact, but turn back and try to rectify my failure.

The rest of the day was gloomy as I alternately taunted and feebly excused myself. The fugitive might have been a trespasser or a servant; his fault might have been slowness, rudeness, theft or attempted murder. Whatever it was, any retaliation the white man chose could be inflicted with impunity. He would not be punished or even tried for it. Popular opinion was unanimous for Negro emigration to Africa, voluntary or forced; those who went westward to join the unconquered Sioux or Nez Perce were looked upon as depraved. Any Negro who didnt embark for Liberia or Sierra Leone, regardless of whether he had the fare or not, deserved anything that happened to him in the United States.

It was because I held, somewhat vaguely, a stubborn refusal to accept this conventional view, a refusal never precisely reasoned and little more, perhaps, than romantic rebellion against my mother in favor of my disreputable Grandfather Backmaker, that I suffered. I couldnt excuse my failure on the grounds that action would have been considered outrageous. It would not have been considered outrageous by me.

I pushed self-contempt at my passivity aside as best I could and strove to recapture the mood of yesterday, succeeding to some extent as the memory of the scene came back less insistently. I even tried pretending the episode had perhaps not been quite as serious as it seemed, or that the pursued had somehow in the end evaded the pursuer. I could not make what had happened not happen; the best I could do was minimize my culpability.

That night I slept a little way from the road and in the morning started off at dawn. Although I was now little more than twenty miles from the metropolis the character of the country had hardly changed. Perhaps the farms were smaller and closer together, their juxtaposition to the estates more incongruous. But traffic was continual now, with no empty stretches on the roads, and the small towns had horse-drawn cars running on iron tracks embedded in the cobbles.

It was late afternoon when I crossed Spuyten Duyvil Creek to Manhattan. Between me and the city now lay a wilderness of squatters' shacks made of old boards, barrel-staves and other discarded rubbish. Lean goats and mangy cats nosed through rubble heaps of broken glass and earthenware demijohns. Mounds of garbage lay beside aimless creeks struggling blindly for the rivers. As clearly as though it had been proclaimed on signposts this was an area of outcasts and fugitives, of men and women ignored and tolerated by the law so long as they kept within the confines of their horrible slum.

Strange and repugnant as the place was, I hesitated to keep on going and arrive in the city at nightfall, but it seemed unlikely there was a place to sleep among the shacks. Once away from the order and sobriety of the post road one could be lost in the squalid maze; undefined threats of vaguely dreadful fates seemed to rise from it like vapors.

Then the fading light revealed the anomaly of a venerable mansion set far back from the highway, with grounds as yet unusurped by the encroaching stews. The house was in ruins; the surrounding gardens lost in brush and weeds. Evidently a watchman or caretaker guarded its forlorn dignity or had very recently abandoned it; I could not imagine its remaining long without being entirely overrun otherwise.

It was almost fully dark as I made my way cautiously toward the remains of an old summerhouse. Its roof was fallen in and it was densely enclosed by ancient rose-bushes whose thorns, I thought, when they pricked my fingers as I struggled through them, ought to give warning of any intruder. For weatherworthiness this shelter had little advantage over the hovels, yet somehow the fact that it had survived seemed to make it a more secure retreat.

I stretched out on the dank boards and slept fitfully, disturbed by dreams that the old mansion was filled with people from a past time who begged me to save them from the slumdwellers and their house from being further ravaged. Brokenly I protested I was helpless—in true dream manner I then became helpless, unable to move—that I could not interfere with what had to happen; they moaned and wrung their hands and faded away. Still, I slept, and in the morning the cramps in my muscles and the aches in my bones disappeared in the excitement of the remaining miles to the city.

And how suddenly it grew up around me, not as though it was a fixed collection of buildings which I approached, but as if I stood still while the wood and stone, iron and brick, sprang into being all about.

New York, in 1938, had a population of nearly a million, having grown very slowly since the close of the War of Southron Independence. Together with the half million in the city of Brooklyn this represented by far the largest concentration of people in the United States, though of course it could not compare with the great Confederate centers of Washington, now including Baltimore and Alexandria, St Louis, or Leesburg (once Mexico City).

The change from the country and the dreadful slums through which I had passed was startling. Cable-cars whizzed northward as far as Fifty-ninth Street on the west side and all the way to Eighty-seventh on the east, while horse-cars furnished convenient crosstown transportation every few blocks. Express steam trains ran through bridged cuts on Madison Avenue, an engineering achievement of which New Yorkers were vastly proud.

Bicycles, rare around Wappinger Falls, were thick as flies, darting ahead and alongside drayhorses pulling wallowing vans, carts or wagons. Prancing trotters drew private carriages, buggies, broughams, victorias, hansoms, dogcarts or sulkies; neither the cyclists, coachmen nor horses seemed overawed or discommoded by occasional minibiles chuffing their way swiftly and implacably over cobblestones or asphalt.

Incredibly intricate traceries of telegraph wires swarmed overhead, crossing and recrossing at all angles, slanting upward into offices and flats or downward to stores, a reminder that no urban family with pretensions to gentility would be without the clacking instrument in the parlor, that every child learned the Morse code before he could read. Thousands of sparrows considered the wires properly their own; they perched and swung, quarreled and scolded on them, leaving only to satisfy their voracity upon the steaming mounds of horsedung below.

The country boy who had never seen anything more metropolitan than Poughkeepsie was tremendously impressed. Buildings of eight or ten storeys were common, and there were many of fourteen or fifteen, serviced by pneumatic English lifts, that same marvelous invention which permitted the erection of veritable skyscrapers in Washington and Leesburg.

Above them balloons moved gracefully through the air, guided and controlled as skillfully as old-time sailing vessels. These were not entirely novel to me; I had seen more of them than I had minibiles, but never so many as here. In a single hour, gawking upward, I counted seven, admiring how nicely calculated their courses were, for they seldom came so low as to endanger lives beneath by having to throw out sandbags in order to rise. That they could so maneuver over buildings of greatly uneven height showed this to be the air age indeed.

Most exciting of all was the great number of people who walked, rode, or merely stood around on the streets. It seemed hardly believable so many humans could crowd themselves so closely. Beggars pleaded, touts wheedled, peddlers hawked, newsboys shouted, bootblacks chanted. Messengers pushed their way, loafers yawned, ladies shopped, drunks staggered. For long moments I paused, standing stock still, not thinking of going on, merely watching the spectacle.

How far I walked, how many different parts of the city I explored that day, I have no idea. I felt I had hardly begun to fondle the sharp edge of wonder when it was twilight and the gas lamps, lit simultaneously by telegraph sparks, gleamed and shone on nearly every corner. Whatever had been drab and dingy in daylight—and even my eyes had not been blind to the dirt and decay—became in an instant magically enchanting, softened and shadowed into mysterious beauty. I breathed the dusty air with a relish I had never known in the country and felt I was inhaling some elixir for the spirit.

But spiritual sustenance is not quite enough for a seventeen-year-old, especially one who is beginning to be hungry and tired. I was desperately anxious to hoard the three precious dollars in my pocket, for I had little idea how to go about replacing them, once they were spent. I could not do without eating, however, so I stopped in at the first gaslit bakery, buying, after some consideration, a penny loaf, and walked on through the entrancing streets, munching at it and feeling like an historical character.

Now the fronts of the tinugraph lyceums were lit up by porters with long tapers, so that they glowed yellow and inviting, each heralded with a boldly lettered broadside or dashingly drawn cartoon advertising the amusement to be found within. I was tempted to see for myself this magical entertainment of pictures taken so close together they gave the illusion of motion, but the lowest admission price was five cents. Some of the more garish theaters, which specialized in the incredible phonotos—tinugraphs ingeniously combined with a sound-producing machine operated by compressed air, so that the pictures seemed not only to move but to talk—actually charged ten or even fifteen cents for an hour's spectacle.

By this time I ached with tiredness; the insignificant

bundle of shirt and books had become a burden. I was pressed by the question of where to sleep and began thinking more kindly than I would have believed possible of last night's slum. I didnt connect my need with the glass transparencies behind which gaslight shone through the unpainted letters of BEDS, ROOMS, or HOTEL, for my mind was hazily fixed on some urban version of the inn at Wappinger Falls or the Poughkeepsie Commercial House.

I became more and more confused as fatigue blurred impressions of still newer marvels, so that I am not entirely sure whether it was one or a succession of girls who offered delights for a quarter. I know I was solicited by crimps for the Confederate Legion who operated openly in defiance of United States law, and an incredible number of beggars accosted me.

At last I thought of asking directions. But without realizing it I had wandered from the thronged wooden or granite sidewalks of the brightly lit avenues into an unpeopled, darkened area where the buildings were low and frowning, where the flicker of a candle or the yellow of a kerosene lamp in windows far apart were uncontested by any streetlights.

All day my ears had been pressed by the clop of hooves, the rattling of iron tires or the puffing of minibiles; now the empty street was unnaturally still. The suddenly looming figure of another walker seemed the luckiest of chances.

"Excuse me, friend," I said. "Can you tell me where's the nearest inn, or anywhere I can get a bed for the night cheap?"

I felt him peering at me. "Rube, huh? Much money you got?"

"Th— Not very much. That's why I want to find cheap lodging."

"OK, Reuben. Come along."

"Oh, don't trouble to show me. Just give me an idea how to get there."

He grunted. "No trouble, Reuben. No trouble at all."

Taking my arm just above the elbow in a firm grip he steered me along. For the first time I began to feel alarm.

However, before I could attempt to shrug free he had shoved me into the mouth of an alley, discernible only because its absolute blackness contrasted with the relative darkness of the street.

"Wait—" I began.

"In here, Reuben. Soundest night's sleep youve had in a long time. And cheap—it's free."

I started to break loose and was surprised to find he no longer held me. Before I could even begin to think, a terrific blow fell on the right side of my head and I traded the blackness of the alley for the blackness of insensibility.

3. A MEMBER OF THE GRAND ARMY

I WAS RECALLED to consciousness by a smell. More accurately a cacophony of smells. I opened my eyes and shut them against the unbearable pain of light; I groaned at the equally unbearable pain in my skullbones. Feverishly and against my will I tried to identify the walloping odors around me.

The stink of death and rottenness was thick. I knew there was an outhouse—many outhouses—nearby. The ground I lay on, where it was not stony, was damp with the water of endless dishwashings and launderings. The noisomeness of offal suggested that the garbage of many families had never been buried, but left to rot in the alley or near it. In addition there was the smell of death, not the sweetish effluvium of blood, such as any country boy who has helped butcher a bull-calf or hog knows, but the unmistakable stench of corrupt, maggotty flesh. Besides all this there was the spoor of humanity.

A new discomfort at last forced my eyes open for the second time. A hard surface was pressing painful knobs into my exposed skin. I looked and felt around me.

The knobs were the scattered cobbles of a fetid alley; not a foot away was the cadaver of a dog, thoroughly putrescent; beyond him a drunk retched and groaned. A trickle of liquid swill wound its way delicately over the moldy earth between the stones. My coat, shirt, and shoes were gone, so was the bundle with my books. There was no use searching my pocket for the three dollars. I knew I was lucky the robber had left me my pants and my life.

22

A middleaged man, at least he looked middleaged to my youthful eye, regarded me speculatively over the head of the drunk. A pale, elliptical scar interrupted the wrinkles on his forehead, its upper point making a permanent part in his thin hair. Tiny red veins marked his nose; his eyes were bloodshot.

"Pretty well cleaned yuh out, huh boy?"

I nodded—and then was sorry for the motion.

"Reward of virtue. Assuming you was virtuous, which I assume. Come to the same end as me, stinking drunk. Only I still got my shirt. Couldnt hock it no matter how thirsty I got."

I groaned.

"Where yuh from boy? What rural—see, sober now—precincts miss you?"

"Wappinger Falls, near Poughkeepsie. My name's Hodge Backmaker."

"Well now, that's friendly of you, Hodge. I'm George Pondible. Periodic. Just tapering off."

I hadnt an idea what Pondible was talking about. Trying to understand made my head worse.

"Took everything, I suppose? Havent a nickel left to help a hangover?"

"My head," I mumbled, quite superfluously.

He staggered to his feet. I slowly sat up, tenderly touching the lump over my ear with my fingertips.

"Best thing—souse it in the river. Take more to fix mine."

"But . . . can I go through the streets like this?"

"Right," he said. "Quite right."

He stooped down and put one hand beneath the drunk, who murmured unintelligibly. With the other he removed the jacket, a maneuver betraying practice, for it elicited no protest from the victim. He then performed the still more delicate operation of depriving him of his shirt and shoes, tossing them all to me. They were a loathsome collection of rags not fit to clean a manurespreader. The jacket was torn and greasy, the pockets hanging like the ears of a dog; the shirt was a filthy tatter, the shoes shapeless fragments of leather with great gapes in the soles.

"It's stealing," I protested.

"Right. Put them on and let's get out of here."

The short walk to the river was through streets lacking the glamour of those of the day before. The tenements were smokestreaked, with steps between the parting bricks where mortar had fallen out; great hunks of wall were kept in place only by the support of equally crazy ones abutting. The wretched things I wore were better suited than Pondible's to this neighborhood, though his would have marked him tramp and vagrant in Wappinger Falls.

The Hudson too was soiled, with an oily scum and debris, so that I hesitated to dip even the purloined shirt, much less my aching head. But urged on by Pondible I climbed down the slimy stones between two docks and pushing the flotsam aside, ducked myself in the unappetizing water.

"Fixes your head," said Pondible with more assurance than accuracy. "Now for mine."

The sun was hot and the shirt dried on my back as we walked away from the river, the jacket over my arm. Now that my mind was clearing my despair grew rapidly; for a moment I wished I had waded farther into the Hudson and drowned.

Admitting any plans I'd had were nebulous and impractical, they had yet been plans of a kind, something in which I could put, or force, my hopes. My appearance had been presentable, I had the means to keep myself fed and sheltered for a few weeks at least. Now everything was changed, any future was gone, literally knocked out of existence and I had nothing to look forward to, nothing on which to exert my energies and dreams. To go back to Wappinger Falls was out of the question, not simply to dodge the bitterness of admitting defeat so quickly, but because I knew how relieved my mother and father must have been to be freed of my uselessness. Yet I had nothing to expect in the city except starvation or a life of petty crime.

Pondible guided me into a saloon, a dark, secretive place, gaslit even this early, with a steam piano tinkling the popular, mournful tune, *Mormon Girl:*

There's a girl in the state of Deseret
I love and I'm trying to for-get.
Forget her for my tired feet's sake
Don't wanna walk to the Great Salt Lake.
They ever build that railroad toooo the ocean
I'd return my Mormon girl's devotion.
But the tracks stop short in Ioway . . .

I couldnt remember the next line. Something about In-
juns say.

"Shot," Pondible ordered the bartender, "and buttermilk for my chum here."

The bartender kept on polishing the wood in front of
him with a wet, dirty rag. "Got any jack?"

"Pay you tomorrow, friend."

The bartender's uninterrupted industry said clearly,
then drink tomorrow.

"Listen," argued Pondible; "I'm tapering off. You know
me. Ive spent plenty of money here."

The bartender shrugged. "I don't own the place; anything goes over the bar has to be rung up on the cash
register."

"Youre lucky to have a job that pays wages."

"Times I'm not so sure. Why don't you indent?"

Pondible looked shocked. "At my age? What would a
company pay for a wornout old carcass? A hundred dollars at the top. Then a release in a couple of years with a
med holdback so I'd have to report every week somewhere.
No, friend, Ive come through this long a free man—in a
manner of speaking—and I'll stick it out. Let's have that
shot; you can see for yourself I'm tapering off. Youll get
your jack tomorrow."

I could see the bartender was weakening; each refusal
was less surly and at last, to my astonishment, he set out a
glass and bottle for Pondible and an earthenware mug of
buttermilk for me. To my astonishment, I say, for credit
was rarely extended on any scale, large or small. The inflation, though sixty years in the past, had left indelible
impressions; people paid cash or did without. Debt was
not only disgraceful, it was dangerous; the notion things

could be paid for while, or even after, they were being used was as unthinkable as was the idea of circulating paper money instead of silver or gold.

I drank my buttermilk slowly, gratefully aware Pondible had ordered the most filling and sustaining liquid in the saloon. For all his unprepossessing appearance and peculiar moral notions, my new acquaintance seemed to have a rude wisdom as well as a rude kindliness.

He swallowed his whiskey and called for a quart pot of light beer which he sipped slowly. "That's the trick of it, Hodge. Avoid the second shot. If you can." He sipped again. "Now what?"

"What?" I repeated.

"Now what are you going to do? What's your aim in life anyway?"

"None—now. I . . . wanted to learn. To study."

He frowned. "Out of books?"

"How else?"

"Books is mostly written and printed in foreign countries."

"There might be more written here if more people had time to learn."

Pondible wiped specks of froth from his beard with the back of his hand. "Might and mightnt. Oh, some of my best friends are book-readers, don't get me wrong, boy."

"I'd thought," I burst out, "I'd thought to try Columbia College. To offer—to beg to be allowed to do any kind of work for tuition."

"Hmm. I doubt it would have worked."

"Anyway I can't go now, looking like this."

"Might be as well. We need fighters, not readers."

" 'We?' "

He did not explain. "Well, you could always take the advice our friend here gave me and indent. A young healthy lad like you could get yourself a thousand or twelve hundred dollars—"

"Sure. And be a slave for the rest of my life."

"Oh, indenting aint slavery. It's better. And worse. For one thing the company buys you won't hold you after you arent worth your keep. Not that long, on account of book-keeping; they lose when they break even. So they cancel your indenture without a cent payment. Course theyll take a med holdback so as to get a dollar or two for your corpse, but that's a long time away for you."

An inconceivably long time. The medical holdback was the least of my distaste, though it had played a large part in the discussions at home. My mother had heard that cadavers for dissection were shipped to foreign medical schools like so much cargo. She was shocked not so much at the thought of the scientific use of her dead body as at its disposal outside the United States.

"Yes," I said. "A long time away. So I wouldnt be a slave for life; just thirty or forty years. Till I wasnt any good to anyone, including myself."

He seemed to be enjoying himself as he drank his beer. "Youre a gloomy gus, Hodge. Taint's bad's that. Indenting's pretty strictly regulated. That's the idea anyway. I aint saying the big companies don't get away with a lot. You can't be made to work over sixty hours a week. Ten hours a day. With twelve hundred dollars you could get all the education you want in your spare time and then turn your learning to account by making enough to buy yourself free."

I tried to think about it dispassionately, though goodness knows I'd been over the ground often enough. It was true the amount, a not improbable one, would see me through college. But Pondible's notion of turning my "learning to account" I knew to be a fantasy. Perhaps in the Confederate States or the German Union knowledge was rewarded with wealth, or at least a comfortable living, but any study I pursued—I knew my own "impracticality" well enough by now—was bound to yield few material benefits in the backward United States, which existed as a nation at all only on the sufferance and unresolved rivalries of the great powers. I'd be lucky to struggle through school and eke out some kind of living as a freeman; I could hardly hope to earn enough to buy back an indenture on what was left of my time after subtracting sixty hours a week.

"It wouldnt work," I said despondently.

Pondible nodded, as though this were the conclusion he had expected me to come to. "Well then," he said, "there's the gangs."

I looked my horror.

He laughed. "Forget your country rearing. What's right? What the strongest country or the strongest man says it is. The government says gangs are wrong, but the government aint strong enough to stop them. And maybe they don't do as much killing as people think. Only when somebody works against them—just like the government. Sure they have to be paid off, but it's just like taxes. If you leave the parsons' sermons out of it there's no difference joining the gangs than the army—if we had one—or the Confederate Legion—"

"They tried to recruit me yesterday. Are they always so . . ."

"Bold?" For the first time Pondible looked angry and I thought the scar on his forehead turned whiter. "Yes, damn them. The Legion must be half United States citizens. When they have to put down a disturbance or run some little cockroach country they send off the Confederate Legion—made up of men who ought to be the backbone of an army of our own."

"But the police—don't they ever try to stop them?"

"What'd I tell you about right being what the strongest country says it is? Sure we got laws against recruiting into a foreign army. So we squawk. And what have we got to back it up with? So the Confederate Legion goes right on recruiting the men who have to beg for a square meal in their own country. Well, the government is pretty near as bad off when it comes to the gangs. Best it can do is pick off some of the little ones and forget about the big ones. Most of the gangsters never even get shot at. They all live high, high as anybody in the twenty-six states, and every so often there's a dividend—more than a workman makes in a lifetime."

I began to be sure my benefactor was a gangster. And yet . . . if this were so why had he wheedled credit from the barkeep? Was it simply an elaborate blind? It seemed hardly worth it.

"A dividend," I said, "or a rope."

"Most gangsters die of old age. Or competition. Aint one been hung I can think of the last five-six years. But I see youve no stomach for it. Tell me, Hodge—you Whig or Populist?"

The sudden change of subject bewildered me. "Why . . . Populist, I guess."

"Why?"

"Oh . . . I don't know . . ." I thought of some of the discussions that used to go on among the men around the smithy. "The Whigs' 'Property, Protection, Permanent Population'—what does it mean to me?"

"Tell you, boy, means this: Property for the Confederates who own factories here and don't want to pay taxes. Protection for foreign capital to come in and buy or hire. Permanent Population—cheap native labor. Build up a prosperous employing class."

"Yes, I know. I can't see how it helps. Ive heard Whigs at home say the money's bound to seep down from above, but it seems awfully roundabout. And not very efficient."

He reached over and clapped me lightly on the shoulder. "That's my boy," he said. "They can't fool you."

I wasnt entirely pleased by his commendation. "And protection means paying more for things than theyre worth."

"Taint only that, Hodge, it's a damn lie as well. Whigs never even tried protection when they was in. Didnt dast. Knew the other countries wouldnt let them."

"As for 'permanent population' . . . well, those who can't make a living are going to go on emigrating to prosperous countries. Permanent population means dwindling population if it means anything."

"Ah," he said. "You got a head on your shoulders, Hodge. Youre all right; books won't hurt you. But what about emigrating? Yourself, I mean?"

I shook my head.

He nodded, chewing on a soggy corner of his mustache. "Don't want to leave the old ship, huh?"

I don't suppose I would have put it exactly that way, or even fully formulated the thought. I was willing to exchange the familiar for the unknown—up to a certain point. The thought of giving up the country in which I'd been born was repugnant. Call it loyalty, or a sense of having ties with the past, or just stubbornness. "Something like that," I said.

"Well now, let's see what weve got." He stuck up a dirty and slightly tremulous hand, turning down a finger as he stated each point. "One, patriot; two, Populist; three, don't like indenting; four, prosperity's got to come from the poor upward, not the rich down." He hesitated, holding his thumb. "You heard of the Grand Army?"

"Who hasnt? Not much difference between them and the regular gangs."

"Now what makes you say that?"

"Why . . . everybody knows it."

"Do, huh? Maybe they know it all wrong. Look here now—and remember about the Confederate Legion riding over the laws of the United States—what would you think ought to be done about foreigners from the strong countries who come here and walk all over us? Or the Whigs who do their dirty work for them?"

"I don't know," I said. "Not murder, certainly."

"Murder," he repeated. "That's a word, Hodge. Means what you want it to mean. Wasnt murder back during the War when Union soldiers was trying to keep the country from being split up. Taint murder today when somebody's hung for rape or counterfeiting. Anyhow the Grand Army don't go in for murder."

I said nothing.

"Oh, accidents happen; wouldnt deny it. Maybe they get a little rougher than they intend with Whig traitors or Confederate agents, but you can't make bacon out of a live hog. Point is the Grand Army's the only thing in the country that even tries to restore it to what it once was. What was fought for in the War."

I don't know whether it was the thought of Grandfather Backmaker or the unassuaged guilt for the miserable figure I had cut only three days back that made me ask, "And do they want to give the Negroes equality?"

He drew back sharply, shock showing clearly on his

face. "Touch of the tarbrush in you, boy? By—" He bent forward, looking at me searchingly. "No, I can see you aint. Just some notions youll outgrow. You just don't understand. We might have won that war if it hadnt been for the Abolitionists."

Would we? I'd heard it said often enough; it would have been presumptuous to doubt it.

"The darkies are better off among their own," he said; "they never should have been here in the first place; black and white can't mix. Leave ideas like that alone, Hodge; there's plenty and enough to be done. Chase the foreigners out, teach their flunkies a lesson, build the country up again."

"Are you trying to get me to join the Grand Army?"

Pondible finished his beer. "Won't answer that one, boy. Let's say I just want to get you somewheres to sleep, three meals a day, and some of that education youre so fired up about. Come along."

4. TYSS

*H*E TOOK ME to a bookseller's and stationery store on Astor Place with a printshop in the basement and the man to whom he introduced me was the owner, Roger Tyss. I spent almost six years there, and when I left neither the store nor its contents nor Tyss himself seemed to have changed or aged.

I know books were sold and others bought to take their places on the shelves or to be piled towerwise on the floor. I helped cart in many rolls of sulphide paper and bottles of printers' ink, and delivered many bundles of damp pamphlets, broadsides, letterheads and envelopes. Inked ribbons for typewriting machines, penpoints, ledgers and daybooks, rulers, paperclips, legal forms and cubes of indiarubber came and went. Yet the identical, invincible disorder, the synonymous dogeared volumes, the indistinguishable stock, the unaltered cases of type seemed fixed for six years, all covered by the same film of dust which responded to vigorous sweeping only by rising into the air and immediately settling back on precisely the same spots.

Roger Tyss grew six years older and I can only charge it to the heedless eye of youth that I saw no signs of that aging. Like Pondible and, as I learned, so many members of the Grand Army, he wore a beard. His was closely trimmed, wiry and grizzled. Above the beard and across his forehead were many fine lines which always held some of the grime of the store or printing press. You did not dwell long on either beard or wrinkles however; what held you were his eyes: large, dark, fierce and compassionate. You might have dismissed him at first glance as simply

an undersized, stoopshouldered, slovenly printer, had it not
been for those eyes which seemed in perpetual conflict
with his other features.

"Robbed and bludgeoned, ay?" he said with a curious
disrespect for sequence after Pondible had explained me
to him. "Dog eats dog, and the survivors survive. Backmaker, ay? Is that an American name?"

So far as I knew, I said, it was.

"Well, well; let's not pry too deeply. So you want to
learn. Why?"

"Why?" The question was too big for an answer, yet an
answer of some kind was expected. "I guess because
there's nothing else so important."

"Wrong," he said triumphantly, "wrong and illusory.
Since nothing is ultimately important there can be no
degrees involved. Books are the waste-product of the human mind."

"Yet you deal in them," I ventured.

"I'm alive and I shall die too; this doesnt mean I approve of either life or death. Well, if you are going to learn
you are going to learn; there's nothing I can do about it.
As well here as another place."

"Thank you, sir."

"Gratitude, Hodgins"—he never then nor later conde-
scended to the familiar "Hodge" nor did I ever address or
even think of him except as Mr Tyss—"Gratitude, Hodgins, is an emotion disagreeable both to the giver and to
the receiver. We do what we must; gratitude, pity, love,
hate, all that cant, is superfluous."

I considered this statement reflectively.

"Look you," he went on, "I'll feed you and lodge you,
teach you to set type and give you the run of the books.
I'll pay you no money; you can steal from me if you must.
You can learn as much here in four months as in a college
in four years—if you persist in thinking it's learning you
want—or you can learn nothing. I'll expect you to do the
work I think needs doing; any time you don't like it youre
free to go."

And so our agreement, if so simple and unilateral a
statement can be called an agreement, was made within

ten minutes after he met me for the first time. For six years the store was home and school, and Roger Tyss was employer, teacher and father to me. He was never my friend. Rather he was my adversary. I respected him and the longer I knew him the deeper became my respect, but it was an ambivalent feeling and attached only to those qualities which he himself would have scorned. I detested his ideas, his philosophy and many of his actions, and this detestation grew until I was no longer able to live near him. But I am getting ahead of my story.

Tyss knew books, not merely as a bookman knows them —binding, size, edition, value—but as a scholar. He seemed to have read enormously and on every conceivable subject, many of them quite useless in practical application. (I remember a long discourse on heraldry, filled with terms like "paley-bendy or," "fusils conjoined in fess, gules" and "sable demi-lions." He regarded such erudition, indeed any erudition, contemptuously. When I asked why he had bothered to pick it up, his retort was, "Why have you bothered to pick up calluses, Hodgins?")

As a printer he followed the same pattern; he was not concerned solely with setting up a neat page; he sometimes spent hours laying out some trivia, which could have interested only its author, until he struck a proof which satisfied him. He wrote much on his own account: poetry, essays, manifestoes, composing directly from the font, running off a single proof which he read—always expressionlessly—and immediately destroyed before pieing the type.

I slept on a mattress kept under one of the counters during the day; Tyss had a couch hardly more luxurious, downstairs by the flatbed press. Each morning before it was time to open he sent me across town on the horse-cars to the Washington Market to buy six pounds of beef— twelve on Saturdays, for the market, unlike the bookstore, was closed Sundays. It was always the same cut, heart of ox or cow, dressed by the butcher in thin strips. After I had been with him long enough to tire of the fare, but not long enough to realize the obstinacy of his nature, I begged him to let me substitute pork or mutton, or at least some other part of the beef, like brains or tripe which were even cheaper. He always answered, "The heart, Hodgins. Purchase the heart; it is the vital food."

While I was on my errand he would buy three loaves of yesterday's bread, still tolerably fresh; when I returned he took a long two-pronged fork, our only utensil, for the establishment was innocent of either cutlery or dishes, and spearing a strip of heart held it over the gas flame of a light standard until it was sooted and toasted rather than broiled. We tore the loaves with our fingers and with a hunk of bread in one hand and a strip of heart in the other we each ate a pound of meat and half a loaf of bread for breakfast, dinner, and supper.

"Man is uniquely a savage eater of carrion," he informed me, chewing vigorously. "What lion or tiger would relish another's ancient, putrefying kill? What vulture or hyena displays human ferocity? Too, we are cannibals at heart. We eat our gods; we have always eaten our gods."

"Isnt that figurative, or poetic, Mr Tyss? I mean, doesnt it refer to the grain of wheat which is 'killed' by the harvester and buried by the sower?"

"You think the gods were modelled on John Barleycorn and not John Barleycorn on them—to conceal their fate? I fear you have a higher opinion of mankind than is warranted, Hodgins."

"I'm not sure I know what you mean by gods."

"Embodiments or personifications of human aspirations. The good, the true, the beautiful—with winged feet or bull's body."

"How about . . . oh, Chronos? Or Satan?"

He licked his fingers of the meat juices, obviously pleased. "Satan. An excellent example. Epitome of man's futile longing to upset and defy the divine plan—I use the word 'divine' derisively, Hodgins—; who does not admire and reverence Lucifer in his heart? Well, having made a god out of the devil we eat him daily in a two-fold sense: by swallowing the myth of his enmity (a truer friend there never was), and by digesting his great precepts of pride and curiosity and strength. And you see for yourself how he finds interesting thoughts for idle minds to speculate on. Let's get to work."

He expected me to work, but he was far from a hard or inconsiderate master. In 1938-44, when the country was being ground deeper into colonialism, there were few employers so lenient. I read much, generally when I pleased, and despite his jeers at learning in the abstract he encouraged me, even going to the length, if a particular book was not to be found in his considerable stock, of letting me get it from one of his competitors, to be written up against his account.

Nor was he scrupulous about the time I took on his errands. I continued to ramble and sight-see the city much as though I had nothing else to do. And if, from time to time, I discovered there were girls in New York who didnt look too unkindly on a tall youth even though he still carried some of the rustic air of Wappinger Falls, he never questioned why the walk of half a mile took me a couple of hours.

True, he kept to his original promise never to pay me wages, but he often handed me coins for pocketmoney, evidently satisfied I wasnt stealing, and he replaced my makeshift wardrobe with worn but decent clothing.

He had not exaggerated the possibilities of the books surrounding me. His brief warning, "—you can learn nothing," was lost on me. I suppose a different temperament might have become surfeited with paper and print; I can only say I wasnt. I nibbled, tasted, gobbled books. After the store was shut I hooked a student lamp to the nearest gasjet by means of a long tube, and lying on my pallet with a dozen volumes handy, I read till I was no longer able to keep my eyes open or understand the words. Often I woke in the morning to find the light still burning and my fingers holding the pages open.

I think one of the first books to influence me strongly was the monumental *Causes of American Decline and Decay* by the always popular expatriate historian, Henry Adams. I was particularly impressed by the famous passage in which he reproves the "stay-at-home" Bostonian essayists, William and Henry James, for their quixotic sacrifice and espousal of a long-lost cause. History, said Sir Henry, who had renounced his United States citizenship and been knighted by William V, history is never directed or diverted by well-intentioned individuals; it is the product of forces with geographical, not moral roots.

Possibly the learned expatriate was right, but my instinctive sympathies lay with the Jameses, in spite of the fact that I had not found their books enjoyable. This was due at least partly to the fact that the small editions were badly printed and marred, at least so foreign critics claimed, by an excessive use of Yankee colloquialisms, consciously employed to demonstrate patriotism and disdain of imported elegance. For some reason, obscure to me then, I did not mention Adams to Tyss, though I usually turned to him with each of my fresh discoveries. When he came upon me with an open book he would glance at the running title over my shoulder and begin talking, either of the particular work or of its topic. What he had to say gave me an insight I might otherwise have missed, and turned me to other writers, other aspects. He respected no authority simply because it was acclaimed or established; he prodded me to examine every statement, every hypothesis no matter how commonly accepted.

Early in my employment I was attracted to a large framed parchment he kept hanging, slightly askew and highly attractive to dust, over his typecase. It was simply but beautifully printed in 16 point Baskerville; I knew without being told that he had set it himself:

The Body of
Benjamin Franklin
Printer
Like the Cover of an Old Book
Stripped of Its Lettering and Gilding
Lies Here
Food for Worms.
But the Work Shall Not Be Lost
For it will, As he Believed,
Come Forth Again
In a new and Better Edition
Revised & Corrected
By
The Author.

When he caught me admiring it Tyss laughed. "Felicitous, isnt it, Hodgins? But a lie, a perverse and probably hypocritical lie. There is no Author; the book of life is simply a mess of pied type, a tale told by an idiot, full of sound and fury, signifying nothing. There is no plan, no synopsis to be filled in with pious hopes or sanctimonious actions. There is nothing but a vast emptiness in the universe."

"The other day you told me we admired the devil for rebelling against a plan."

He grinned. "So you expect consistency instead of truth from me, Hodgins. There is no plan, authored by a Mind; it is this no-plan against which Lucifer fought. But there is a plan too, a mindless plan, which accounts for all our acts."

I had been reading an obscure Irish theologian, a Protestant curate of some forsaken parish, so ill-esteemed he had been forced to publish his sermons himself, named George B Shaw, and I had been impressed by his forceful style. I quoted him to Tyss, perhaps as much to preen myself as to counter his argument.

"Nonsense. Ive seen the good parson's book with its eighteenth-century logic and its quaint rationalism, and know it for a waste of ink and paper. Man does not think; he only thinks he thinks. An automaton, he responds to external stimuli; he cannot order his thought."

"You mean that there's no free will? Not even a marginal minimum of choice?"

"Exactly. The whole thing is an illusion. We do what we do because someone else has done what he did; he did it because still another someone did what he did. Every action is the rigid result of another action."

"But there must have been a beginning," I objected. "And if there was a beginning, choice existed if only for that split second. And if choice exists once it can exist again."

"You have the makings of a metaphysician, Hodgins," he said witheringly, for metaphysics was one of the most despised words in his vocabulary. "The reasoning is infantile. Answering you and the Reverend Shaw on your own level, I could say that time is a convention and that all events occur simultaneously. Or if I grant its dimension I can ask, What makes you think time is a simple straight line running flatly through eternity? Why do you assume that time isnt curved? Can you conceive of its end? Can you really imagine its beginning? Of course not; then why arent both the same? The serpent with its tail in its mouth?"

"You mean we not only play a prepared script but repeat the identical lines over and over and over for infinity? There's no heaven in your cosmos, only an unimaginable, never-ending hell."

He shrugged his shoulders. "That you should spout emotional apologetics at me is part of what you call the script, Hodgins. You didnt select the words nor speak them voluntarily. They were called into existence by what I said, which in turn was mere response to what went before."

Weakly I was forced back to a more elementary attack. "You don't act in accordance with your own conviction."

He snorted. "A thoughtless remark, excusable only because automatic. How could I act differently? Like you, I am a prisoner of stimuli."

"How pointless to risk ruin and imprisonment as a member of the Grand Army when no one can change what's predestined."

"Pointless or not, emotions and reflections are responses just as much as actions. I can no more help engaging myself in the underground than I can help breathing, or my heart beating, or dying when the time comes. Nothing, they say, is certain but death and taxes; actually everything is certain. Everything," he repeated firmly.

I went back to sorting some pamphlets which were to be sold for wastepaper, shaking my head. His theory was unassailable; every attack was discounted by the very nature of the thesis. That it was false I didnt doubt; its impregnability made its falseness still more terrifying.

There were fully as many imaginary discussions with Tyss as real ones. Yet even in these disembodied arguments I could gain no advantage. Why do you look back on the War of Southron Independence with regret for what might have been, if no might-have-been is possible? I asked him mentally, knowing his answer, I cannot help myself, was no answer at all.

The logical illogic of it was only one of the multitude of contradictions in him. The Grand Army to which he was devoted was a violent organization of violent men. He himself was an advocate and implement of violence—one illegal paper, the *True American,* came from his press and I often saw crumpled proofs of large type warnings to "Get Out of Town you Conf. TRAITOR or the GA will HANG YOU!" Yet cruelty, other than intellectually, was repugnant to him; his vindictiveness toward the Whigs and Confederates rose from commiseration for the condition into which they had plunged the country.

Pondible and the others who bore an indefinable resemblance to each other, bearded or not, came to the store on Grand Army business, and I was sure many of the errands I was sent on advanced or were supposed to advance the Grand Army's cause. Those who signed receipts with an X—and in the beginning at least Tyss was strict about assurance of delivery—seemed unlikely customers for the sort of merchandise we handled.

I was relieved, but puzzled and perhaps a little piqued, that aside from the very first conversation with Pondible, no attempt was made to persuade me into the organization. Tyss must have perceived this, for he explained obliquely.

"There's the formative type, Hodgins, and the spectator type. One acts, and the other is acted upon. One changes events, the other observes them. Of course," he went on hastily, "I'm not talking metaphysical rubbish. When I say the formative type changes events I merely mean he reacts to a given stimulus in a positive way while the spectator reacts to the same circumstances negatively, both reactions being inevitable and inescapable. Naturally, events are never changed."

"Why can't one be one type sometimes and the other at other times? Ive certainly heard of men of action who have sat down to write their memoirs."

"You are confusing the after-effect of action with nonaction, the dying ripples on a pond into which a stone has been tossed with the still surface of one which has never been disturbed. No, Hodgins, the two types are completely distinct and unchangeable. The Swiss police chief, Carl Jung, has refined and improved the classifications of Lombroso, showing how the formative type can always be detected."

I felt he was talking pure nonsense, even though I had never read Lombroso or heard of Chief Jung.

"To the formative type the spectator seems useless, to the spectator the man of action is faintly absurd. A born observer would find the earnest efforts of the Grand Army —the formation of skeleton companies, the appointment of officers, the secret drills, the serious attempt to become a real army—lacking in humor and repellent."

"You think I'm the spectator type, Mr Tyss?"

"No doubt about it, Hodgins. Certain features might be deceptive at first sight: the wide-spaced eyes, the restrained fleshiness of the mouth, the elevation of the nostril; but they subordinate to more subtle indicators. No question but that Chief Jung would put you down as an observer."

If his fantastic reasoning and curious manner of classifying personalities as though they were zoological specimens could relieve me of having to refuse pointblank to join the Grand Army I was content. While this hardly alleviated my disturbance at being, no matter how remotely, accessory to mayhem, kidnaping and murder I compromised with my conscience by trying to believe I might after all be mistaken in thinking I was being used. There were times when I felt I ought boldly to declare myself and leave the store but when I faced the prospect of having to find a way to eat and sleep, even if I put aside the imperative necessity of books, I lacked the courage.

Spectator? Why not? Spectators had no difficult decisions to make.

5. OF WHIGS AND POPULISTS

A COUNTRY DEFEATED in a bitter war and divested of half its territory loses its drive and spirit and suffers a shock which is communicated to all its people. For generations its citizens brood over what has happened, preoccupied with the past and dreaming of a miraculous change, until time brings apathy or a reversal of history. The Grand Army, with its crude and brutal philosophy and methods, was pride's answer to defeat.

It was not the only answer; the two major political parties had others. The realistic Whigs wanted to fit the country and its economy into actual world conditions, to subordinate it wholly and openly to the great manufacturing nations and accept with gratitude foreign capital and foreign protection. The immediate result would be more prosperity for the propertied classes; they contended this would mean a gradual raising of the standard of living since employers could hire more hands, and indenture, faced by competition with wages, would dwindle away.

This the Populists denied. The government, they insisted when they were out of office, should create industries, forbid indenting, buy up the indentures of skilled workers and offer high enough pay to create new markets, and defy the world by building a new army and navy. That they never put their program into effect they laid to the wily tricks of the Whigs.

The presidential election of 1940 was as violent as if the office were really a prize to be sought rather than a practically empty title, with all real power now held by the

42

Majority Leader of the House and his cabinet of Committee Chairmen. As early as May one of the leading contenders for the Populist nomination was shot and badly crippled; the Cleveland hall where the Whig convention was being held was fired by an arsonist.

I would not be old enough to vote for two years, yet I too had campaign fever. Jennings Lewis, the Populist, was perhaps the ugliest candidate ever offered, with a hairless, skeletonlike face; Dewey, the Whig nominee, had a certain handsomeness, which might have been an asset if the persistent advocates of woman suffrage had ever gotten their way.

Traditionally, candidates never ventured west of Chicago, concentrating their appearances in New York and New England and leaving the campaign in the sparsely settled trans-Mississippi to local politicians. This year both office-seekers used every device to reach the greatest number of voters. Dewey made a grand tour in his balloon-train; Lewis was featured in a series of short phonotos which were shown free. Dewey spoke several times daily to small groups; Lewis specialized in enormous weekly rallies followed by torchlight parades.

One of these Populist rallies was held in Union Square early in September; outgoing President George Norris spoke, and ex-President Norman Thomas, the only Populist to serve two terms since the beloved Bryan. Tyss indulgently gave me permission to leave the store a couple of hours before the meeting was to commence so I might get a place from which to see and hear all that was going on. Though he characterized all elections as meaningless exercises devised to befuddle, he had been active in this one in some mysterious and secretive way.

The square was already well filled when I arrived, with the more acrobatic members of the audience perched on the statues of LaFayette and Washington. Calliopes played patriotic airs, and a compressed air machine shot up puffs of smoke which momentarily spelled out the candidate's name. Resigned to pantomime glimpses of what was going on, I moved around the outside edge of the crowd, thinking I might just as well leave altogether.

"Please don't step on my foot so firmly. Or is that part of the Populist tradition?"

"Excuse me, Miss; I'm sorry. Did I hurt you?"

We were close enough to a light standard for me to see she was young and well-dressed, hardly the sort of girl to be found at a political meeting, few of which ever counted much of a feminine audience.

She rubbed her instep briefly. "It's all right," she conceded grudgingly. "Serves me right for being curious about the mob."

She was plump and pretty, with a small, discontented mouth and pale hair worn long over her shoulders. "There's not much to see from here," I said; "unless youre enthusiastic enough to be satisfied with a bare look at the important people, perhaps you'd let me help you to the streetcar. For my clumsiness."

She looked at me thoughtfully. "I can manage by myself. But if you feel you owe me something for trampling me, maybe you'll explain why anyone comes to these ridiculous gatherings."

"Why . . . to hear the speakers."

"Hardly any of them can. Only those close up."

"Well then, to show their support of the party, I guess."

"That's what I thought. It's a custom or rite or something like that. A stupid amusement."

"But cheap," I said. "And those who vote for Populists usually havent much money."

"Maybe that's why," she answered. "If they found more useful things to do they'd earn money; then they wouldnt vote for Populists."

"A virtuous circle. If everyone voted Whig we'd all be rich as Whigs."

She shrugged her shoulders, a gesture I found pleasing. "It's easy enough to be envious of those who are better off; it's a lot harder to become better off yourself."

"I can't argue with you on that, Miss . . . um . . .?"

"Why Mister Populist, do ladies always tell you their names when you step on their feet?"

"I'm not usually lucky enough to find feet to step on that have lovely ladies attached," I answered boldly. "I won't deny Populist leanings, but my name is really Hodge Back-maker."

Hers was Tirzah Vame, and she was indentured to a family of wealthy Whigs who owned a handsome modern castiron and concrete house near the Reservoir at Forty-second Street and Fifth Avenue. She had used the apt word "curious" in characterizing herself but it was, as I soon found out, a cold and inflexible curiosity which explored only what she thought might be useful or which impressed her as foolish. She was interested in the nature of anything fashionable or popular or much talked of, the idea of being concerned with anything even vaguely abstract struck her as preposterous.

She had indented, not out of stark economic necessity, but calculatedly, believing she could achieve economic security through indenture. This seemed paradoxical to me, even when I contrasted my "free" condition with her bound one. Certainly she seemed to have minimum restriction on her time; soon after our introduction at the rally she was meeting me almost every evening in Reservoir Square where we sat for hours talking on a bench or walking briskly when the autumn weather chilled our blood.

I did not long flatter myself that her interest—perhaps tolerance would be a better word—was due to any strong attraction exerted by me. If anything she was, I think, slightly repelled by my physical presence, which carried to her some connotation of ordinary surroundings and contrasted with the well-fed smooth surfaces of her employers and their friends. The first time I kissed her she shuddered slightly; then, closing her eyes, she allowed me to kiss her again.

She did not resist me when I pressed my lovemaking; she led me quietly to her room in the big house on my transparent plea that the outdoors was now too cold even for conversation. I was no accomplished seducer, but even in my awkward eagerness I could see she had made up her mind I was to succeed.

That her complaisance was not the result of passion was soon obvious; there was not so much a failure on my part to arouse her as a refusal on hers to be aroused beyond an inescapable degree. Even as she permitted our intimacy she remained as virginal, aloof and critical as before.

"It seems hardly worth the trouble. Imagine people talking and writing and thinking about nothing else."

"Tirzah dear—"

"And the liberties that seem to go with it. I don't think of you as any more dear than I did an hour ago. If people must indulge in this sort of thing, and I suppose they must since it's been going on for a long time, I think it could be conducted with more dignity."

As my infatuation increased her coolness did not lessen; curiosity alone seemed to move her. She was amused at my pathetic search for knowledge. "What good is your learning ever going to do you? It'll never get you a penny."

I smoothed the long, pale hair and kissed her ear. "Suppose it doesnt?" I argued lazily; "There are other things besides money."

She drew away. "That's what those who can't get it always say."

"And what do people who can get it say?"

"That it's the most important thing of all," she answered earnestly. "That it will buy all the other things."

"It will buy you free of your indenture," I admitted, "but you have to get it first."

"Get it first? I never let it go. I still have the contract payment."

"Then what was the point of indenting at all?"

She looked at me wonderingly. "Havent you ever thought about serious things? Only books and politics and all that? How could I get opportunities without indenting? I doubt if the Vames are much of a cut above the Backmakers; well, youre a general drudge and I'm a governess and tutor and even in a way a sort of distant friend to Mrs Smythe."

"That sounds suspiciously like snobbery to me."

"Does it? Well, I'm a snob; Ive never denied it. I want to live like a lady, to have a good house with servants and carriages and minibiles, to travel to civilized countries, with a place in Paris or Rome or Vienna. You can love the poor and cheer for the Populists; I love the rich and the Whigs."

"That's all very well," I objected, "but even though you have your indenting money and can buy back your freedom any moment you want it, how does this help you get rich?"

"Do you think I keep my money in my pocket? It's invested, every cent. People who come to this house give me tips; not just money, though there's enough of that to add a bit to my original capital, but tips on what to buy and sell. By the time I'm thirty I should be well off. Of course I may marry a rich man sooner."

"That's an awfully cold-blooded way of looking at marriage," I remonstrated.

"Is it?" she asked indifferently. "Well, youve been telling me I'm cold-blooded anyway. I may as well be cold-blooded profitably."

"If that's the way you feel I don't understand what we're doing here at this moment. I'd have thought you'd have picked a more profitable lover."

She was unruffled. "You didnt think about it at all. If you had, you would have seen I could hardly encourage any of the men from the class into which I intend to marry. Great ladies can laugh at gossip, but the faintest whisper about someone like me would be damaging. Scandal would be unavoidable if I appeared to be anything in this house but a chilly prude."

An appearance not too deceitful, I considered, sickly jealous at the thought of men who might have been in my place if they had been as anonymous, as inconsequential as I. But this writhing jealousy was little more painful than my frustration at having been made a convenience, a trial experiment. Almost anyone of equal unimportance, anyone who was not a fellow-servant or a familiar in the house would have done as well as I, anyone unlikely ever to come face to face with Mrs Smythe, much less talk to her.

Looking back, trying to recapture for a moment that vanished past, I have a sad, quizzical welling of pity for the girl Tirzah and the boy Hodge. How gravely we took our moral and political differences; how lightly the flying mo-

ments of union. We said and did all the wrong things, all
the things which fostered the antagonism between us and
none of the things which might have softened our youthful
self-assurance. We wrangled and argued: Dewey and
Lewis, Whig versus Populist, materialist against idealist,
reality opposing principle. It all seems so futile now; it all
appeared so vital then.

Added to the almost unanimous distrust and hatred of all
foreigners in the United States, we regarded the Confederates in particular as the cause of all our misfortunes.
We not only blamed and feared them, but looked upon
them as sinister, so Populist orators had a ready-made response every time they referred to the Whigs as Southron
tools.

Contrary to the accepted view in the United States, I
was sure the victors in the War of Southron Independence
had been men of the highest probity, and the noblest among
them was their second president. Yet I also knew that immediately after the Peace of Richmond less dedicated individuals became increasingly powerful in the new nation.
As Sir John Dahlberg remarked, "Power tends to corrupt."

From his first election in 1865 until his death ten years
later, President Lee had been the prisoner of an increasingly strong and imperialistic congress. He had opposed
the invasion and conquest of Mexico by the Confederacy,
undertaken on the pretext of restoring order during the
conflict between the republicans and the emperor. However
he had too profound a respect for the constitutional proc-
esses to continue this opposition in the face of joint resolutions by the Confederate House and Senate.

Lee remained a symbol, but as the generation which had
fought for independence died, the ideals he symbolized
faded. Negro emancipation, enacted largely because of
pressure from men like Lee, soon revealed itself as a device
for obtaining the benefits of slavery without its obligations.
The freedmen on both sides of the new border were without franchise, and for all practical purposes without civil
rights. Yet while the old Union first restricted and then
abolished immigration, the Confederacy encouraged it,
making the newcomers subjects like the Latin-Americans

who made up so much of the Southron population after the Confederacy expanded southward, limiting full citizenship to posterity of enfranchised residents in the Confederate States on July Fourth 1864.

The Populists claimed the Whigs were Confederate agents; the Whigs retorted that the Populists were visionaries and demagogues who tolerated if they did not actually encourage the activities of the Grand Army. The Populists replied by pointing to their platform which denounced illegal organizations and lawless methods. I was not too impressed by this, knowing how busy Tyss, Pondible and their associates had been ever since the campaign started.

On election night Tyss closed the store and we walked the few blocks to Wanamaker & Stewarts drygoods store where a big screen showed the returns between tinugraphs puffing the firm's merchandise. From the first it was apparent the unpredictable electorate preferred Dewey to Lewis. State after state, hitherto staunchly Populist, turned to the Whigs for the first time since William Hale Thompson defeated President Thomas R Marshall back in 1920 and again Alfred E Smith in 1924, before Smith gained the great popularity which gave him the presidency four years later. Only Massachusetts, Connecticut, Dakotah and Oregon went for Lewis; his own Minnesota along with twenty-one other states plumped for Dewey.

Disappointed as I was, I could not but note Tyss's cheerful air. When I asked him what satisfaction he could find in so overwhelming a defeat he smiled and said, "What defeat, Hodgins? Did you think we wanted the Populists to win? To elect Jennings Lewis with his program of world peace conferences? Really Hodgins, I'm afraid you learn nothing day by day."

"You mean the Grand Army wanted Dewey all along?"

"Dewey or another; we prefer a Whig administration which presents a fixed target to a Populist one wavering all over the place."

Of course it should have occurred to me that Tyss and Tirzah would wind up on the same side. It was a measure of my innocence that it never had.

6. ENFANDIN

*T*IRZAH'S QUESTION, "What good is your learning ever going to do you?" bothered me from time to time. Not that I was burdened by any vast amount of knowledge, but presumably I would get more—and then what? It was true I expected no rewards from reading except the pleasure it gave me, but the future, to use a topheavy word, could not be entirely disregarded. I could not see myself spending a lifetime in the bookstore. I was grateful to Tyss, despite his disdain of this emotion, for the opportunities he had given me, but not grateful enough to reconcile myself to becoming another Tyss, especially one without his vitalizing involvement with the Grand Army.

Other courses were neither numerous nor inviting. To follow Tirzah's own example might have seemed feasible if one ignored the vast differences of situation and character, to say nothing of those between a hulking youth and a pretty girl. I could hardly hope to find a wealthy family who would buy my services, put me to congenial tasks, and look with tolerance on my efforts to advance myself right out of their employment. Even if such a chance existed I could not have utilized it as she did; I should undoubtedly confuse one stock with another or neglect to buy what I was told until too late, winding up with lottery tickets and losing the stubs.

My helpless uncertainty only added to my disadvantage with her. I had no hope her coolness would change to either ardor or affection. At any moment she might decide her curiosity was satisfied and find the awkwardness, inconveniences, and what must have been to her the sordidness of the affair too great.

We were a strange pair of young lovers. When we talked we argued opposing views or spoke sedately of things not near our hearts. When we walked together in the streets or fled the gaslit pavements for the moon over Reservoir Square we neither held hands nor kissed impulsively. Because prudence forbade the slightest physical contact save in utmost privacy there were no innocent touchings or accidental brushing of hands against hips or arms against arms, and our secret embraces were guilty simply because they were secret.

Often I dreamed of a miraculous change, either in circumstances or in her attitude, to dissolve the walls between us; beneath the hope was only expectation of an abrupt and final break. Yet when it came at last, after more than a year, it was not the result, as I had agonizedly anticipated, of some successful speculation or an offer of marriage, but of natural and normal actions of my own.

Among the customers to whom I frequently delivered parcels of books was a Monsieur René Enfandin who lived on Eighth Street, not far from Fifth Avenue. M Enfandin was Consul for the Republic of Haiti; the house he occupied was distinguished from otherwise equally drab neighbors by a large red and blue escutcheon over the doorway. He did not use the entire dwelling himself, reserving only the parlor floor for the office of the consulate and living quarters; the rest was let to other tenants.

Tyss's anti-foreign bias caused him to jeer at Enfandin behind his back and embark on discourses which proved by anthropometry and frequent references to Lombroso and Chief Jung that Negroes were incapable of self-government. I noticed however that he treated the consul no differently, either in politeness or honesty, from his other patrons, and by this time I knew Tyss well enough to attribute this courtesy not to the self-interest of a tradesman but to that compassion which he suppressed so sternly under the contradictions of his nature.

For a long time I paid little attention to Enfandin, beyond noting the wide range of interests revealed by the books he bought. I sensed that, like myself, he was inclined to shyness. He had an arrangement whereby he turned back most of his purchases for credit on others. I saw that if he hadnt, his library would have soon dispossessed him; as it was, books covered all the space not taken by the paraphernalia of his office and bedroom with the exception of a bit of bare wall on which hung a large crucifix. He seemed always to have a volume in his large, dark brown hand, politely closed over his thumb or open for eager sampling.

Enfandin was tall and strong-featured, notable in any company. In the United States where a black man was, more than anything else, a reminder of the disastrous war and Mr Lincoln's proclamation, he was the permanent target of rowdy boys and adult hoodlums. Even the diplomatic immunity of his post was poor protection, for it was believed, not without justification, that Haiti, the only American republic south of the Mason-Dixon line to preserve its independence, was disrupting the official if sporadically executed policy of deporting Negroes to Africa by encouraging their emigration to its own shores or, what was even more annoying, assisting them to flee to the unconquered Indians of Idaho or Montana.

Beyond a "Good morning" or "Thank you" I doubt if we exchanged a hundred words until the time I saw a copy of Randolph Bourne's *Fragment* among his selections. "That's not what you think it is," I exclaimed brashly; "it's a novel."

He looked at me gravely. "You also admire Bourne?"

"Oh yes." I felt a trifle foolish, not only for having thrust my advice upon him, but for the inadequacy of my comment on a writer who had so many pertinent things to say and had been persecuted for saying them. I was conscious too of Tyss's opinion: How could a cripple like Bourne speak to whole and healthy men?

"But you do not approve of fiction, is that so?" Enfandin had no discernible accent but often his English was uncolloquial and sometimes it was overly careful and stiff.

I thought of the adventure tales I had once swallowed so breathlessly. "Well . . . it does seem to be a sort of a waste of time."

He nodded. "Time, yes . . . We waste it or save it or use it—one would almost think we mastered it instead of the other way around. Yet are all novels really a waste of the precious dimension? Perhaps you underestimate the value of invention."

"No," I said; "but what value has the invention of happenings that never happened, or characters who never existed?"

"Who is to say what never happened? It is a matter of definition."

"All right," I said; "suppose the characters exist in the author's mind, like the events; where does the value of the invention come in?"

"Where the value of any invention comes in," he answered. "In its purpose or use. A wheel spinning aimlessly is worth nothing; the same wheel on a cart or a pulley changes destiny."

"You can't learn anything from fairy tales," I persisted stubbornly.

He smiled. "Maybe you havent read the right fairy tales."

I soon discovered in him a quick and penetrating sympathy which was at times almost telepathic. He listened to my callow opinions patiently, offering observations of his own without diffidence and without didacticism. The understanding and encouragement I did not expect or want from Tyss he gave me generously. To him, as I never could to Tirzah, I talked of my hopes and dreams; he listened patiently and did not seem to think them foolish or impossible of accomplishment. I do not minimize what Tyss did for me by saying that without Enfandin I would have taken much less profit from the books my employer gave me access to.

I was drawn to him more and more; I'm not sure why he interested himself in me, unless there was a reason in the remark he made once: "Ay, we are alike, you and I. The books, always the books. And for themselves, not to become rich or famous like sensible people. Are we not foolish? But it is a pleasant folly and a sometimes blameless vice."

I wanted anxiously to speak of Tirzah, not only because it is an urgent necessity for lovers to mention the name at least of their beloved a hundred times a day or more, but in the nebulous hope he could somehow give me an answer to her as well as to her question. I approached the topic in a number of different ways; each time our conversation moved on without my having told him about her.

Often, after I had delivered an armful of books to the consulate and we had talked of a wide range of things— for, unlike me, he had no selfconsciousness about what interested him, whether others might consider it trivial or not—he would walk back to the bookstore with me, leaving a note on his door. The promise that he would be "Back in 10 minutes" was, I'm afraid, seldom fulfilled, for he became so deeply engrossed that he was unaware of time.

The occasion which was to be so important to me sprang from a discussion of non-resistance to evil, a subject on which he had much to say. We were just passing Wanamaker & Stewarts and he had just triumphantly reviewed the amazing decision of the Japanese Shogun to abolish all police forces, when I became conscious that someone was staring fixedly at me.

A minibile, highslung and obviously custom-built, moved slowly down the street. Its brass brightwork, bumpers like two enormous tackheads, hub rims like delicate eyelets in the center of the great spokes, rococo lamps, rain gutters and door handles, was dazzling. In the jump-seat, facing a lady of majestic demeanor, was Tirzah. Her head was turned ostentatiously away from us.

Enfandin halted as I did. "Ah," he murmured; "you know the ladies?"

"The girl. The lady is her employer."

"I caught only a glimpse of the face, but it is a pretty one."

"Yes. Oh yes . . ." I wanted desperately to say more, to thank him as though Tirzah's looks were somehow to my credit, to praise her and at the same time call her cruel and hardhearted. "Oh yes . . ."

"She is perhaps a particular friend?"

I nodded. "Very particular." We walked on in silence.

"That is nice. But she is perhaps a little unhappy over your prospects?"

"How did you know?"

"It was not too hard to infer. You have been concealed from the mistress; the young lady is impressed by wealth; you are the idealistic one who is not."

At last I was able to talk. I explained her indenture, her ambitious plans, and how I expected her to end everything between us at any moment. "And there's nothing I can do about it," I finished bitterly.

"That is right, Hodge. There is nothing you can do about it because— You will forgive me if I speak plainly, brutally even?"

"Go ahead. Tirzah—" what a joy it was just to say the name "—Tirzah has told me often enough how unrealistic I am."

"That was not what I meant. I would say there is nothing you can do about it because there is nothing you wish to do about it."

"What do you mean? I'd do anything I could . . ."

"Would you? Give up books, for instance?"

"Why should I? What good would that do?"

"I do not say you should or that it would do good. I only try to show that the young lady, charming and important as she is, is not the most magnetic or important thing in your life. Romantic love is a curious byproduct of west European feudalism that Africans and Asiatics can only criticize gingerly. You shake your head with obstinacy; you do not believe me. Good, then I have not hurt you."

"I can't see that youve helped me much, either."

"Ay! What did you expect from the black man of Haiti? Miracles?"

"Nothing less will do any good I'm afraid. Now I suppose youll tell me I'll get over it in time; that it's just an adolescent languishing anyway."

He looked at me reproachfully. "No, Hodge. I hope I should never be the one to think suffering is tied to age or time. As for getting over it, why, we all get over everything in the end, but no matter how desirable absolute peace is, few of us are willing to give up experience prematurely."

Later, I compared what Enfandin told me with what Tyss might have said. Did the responsibility of holding Tirzah lie with me and not with both of us, or with fate or chance? Or were events so circumscribed by inevitabilities that even to think of struggling with them was foolish?

I also asked myself if I had been too proud, too hypersensitive. I had tried to make her see my viewpoint by arguing, by fighting hers; might it not be possible, without giving up essentials, to approach her more gently? To divert her, not from her ambitions, but from her contempt for mine?

Full of resolves, I left the store after eight; eager walking brought me to our meeting place in Reservoir Square early, but the nearby churchbells had hardly sounded the quarter hour when she said, "Hodge."

Her unusual promptness was a good omen; I was filled with warm optimism. "Tirzah, I saw you this afternoon—"

"Did you? I thought you were so busy with Sambo you would never look up."

"Why do you call him that? Do you think—"

"Oh for Heavens sake, don't start making speeches at me. I call him Sambo because it sounds nicer than Rastus."

All my resolutions about trying to see her point of view! "I call him M'sieu Enfandin because that's his name."

"Have you no pride? No, I suppose you havent. Just some strange manners. Well, I can put up with your eccentricities, but other people wouldnt understand. What do you think Mrs Smythe would say?"

"Never having met the lady, I havent the faintest idea."

"I have, and I agree with her. Would you like me to be chummy with a naked cannibal with a ring in his nose?"

"But Enfandin doesnt wear a ring in his nose, and you must have seen he was fully dressed. Maybe he eats missionaries in secret, but that couldnt offend Mrs Smythe since appearances would be saved."

"I'm serious, Hodge."

"So am I. Enfandin is my only friend."

"You may be above appearances and considerations of decency but I'm not. If you ever appear in public with him again you can stop coming here. Because I won't have anything more to do with you."

"But Tirzah . . ." I began helplessly, overwhelmed by the impossibility of coping with the irrelevancies and inconsistencies of her stand. "But Tirzah . . ."

"No," she said firmly; "you'll simply have to grow up, Hodge, and stop such childish exhibitions. Only friend indeed! Why I suppose if he appeared here right this minute, you'd talk to him."

"Well naturally. You'd hardly expect me to—"

"But I do. That's exactly what I'd expect. You to act like a civilized man."

I wasnt angry. I couldnt be angry with her. "If that's civilization then I guess I don't want to be civilized."

I detected astonishment in her voice. "You mean, actually mean, you intend to keep on acting this way?"

Grandfather Backmaker must have been a stubborn man; I had my mother's word I possessed no Hodgins traits. "Tirzah, what would you think of me if I turned on my only friend, the only thoroughly kind and understanding friend Ive ever had, just because Mrs Smythe has different notions of propriety than I have?"

"I'd think you were beginning to understand things at last."

"I'm sorry, Tirzah."

"I mean it, Hodge, you know. I'll never see you again."

"If you'd only listen to my side—"

"You mean if I would only become a crank like you. But I don't want to be a crank or a martyr. I don't want to change the world. I'm normal."

"Tirzah—"

"Goodbye, Hodge."

She walked away. I had the irrational feeling that if I called after her she might come back. Or at least stand still and wait to hear what I had to say. I kept my mouth obstinately closed; Enfandin had been right, the responsibility was mine. There were things I would not give up.

My heroic mood must have lasted fully fifteen minutes.

Then I hurried through the little park and across the street to the Smythe house. There were lights in the upper floors, but the basement, as always, was dark. I dared not knock or ring the bell; her admonitions were too firmly impressed on my mind. Instead, in a turmoil of emotions, I paced the flagged sidewalk until the suspicious eye of a patrolman was attracted; then I fled cravenly.

I couldnt wait for the next day to write a long, chaotic letter begging her to let me talk to her, just to talk to her, for an hour, ten minutes, a minute. I offered to indent, to emigrate, to make a fortune by some inspired means if only she would hear me. I recalled moments together, I told her I loved her, said I would die without her. Having covered several pages with these sentiments I began all over and repeated them. It was dawn when I posted the letter in the pneumatic mail.

Sleepless and tormented, I was of little use to Tyss next day. Would she telegraph? If she answered by pneumatic post her letter might be delivered in the afternoon. Or would she come to the bookstore?

The second day I sent off two more letters and went up to Reservoir Square on the chance she might appear. I watched the house as though my concentration would force her to emerge. On the third day my letters came back, unopened.

There is some catchphrase or other about the elasticity of youth. It is true it was only weeks before my misery abated, and weeks more before I was heart-whole again. But those weeks were long.

The subject of Tirzah did not come up again between Enfandi and me. He must have sensed I had lost her, perhaps he even guessed his connection with the break, but he was too tactful to mention it and I was too sore.

I don't know if the episode precipitated some maturity in me, or if, as a result of grief and anger I tried to turn my mind away from the easy emotions and shield myself against further hurt. At any rate, whether there was a logical connection or not, it is from this period that I date my resolve to center my reading on history. Somewhat diffidently I spoke of this to him.

"History? But certainly, Hodge. It is a noble study. But what is history? How is it written? How is it read? Is it a dispassionate chronicle of events scientifically determined and set down in the precise measure of their importance? Is this ever possible? Or is it the transmutation of the ordinary into the celebrated? Or the cunning distortion which gives a clearer picture than accurate blueprints?"

"It seems to me facts are primary and interpretations come after," I answered. "If we can find out the facts we can form our individual opinions on them."

"Perhaps. Perhaps. But take what is for me the central fact of all history." He pointed to the crucifix. "As a Catholic the facts are plain to me; I believe what is written in the Gospels to be literally true: that the Son of Man died for me on that cross. But what were the facts for a contemporary Roman statesman? That an obscure local agitator threatened the stability of an uneasy province and was promptly executed in the approved Roman fashion as a warning to others. And for a contemporary fellow-countryman? That no such person existed. You think these facts are mutually exclusive? Yet you know no two people see exactly the same thing; too many honest witnesses have contradicted each other. Even the Gospels must be reconciled."

"You are saying that truth is relative."

"Am I? Then I shall have my tongue examined, or my head. Because I mean to say no such thing. Truth is absolute and for all time. But one man cannot envisage all of truth; the best he can do is see a single aspect of it whole. That is why I say to you, be a skeptic, Hodge. Always be the skeptic."

"Ay?" I was finding the admonition a little difficult to harmonize with his previous confession of faith.

"For the believer skepticism is essential. How else is he to know false gods from true except by doubting both? One of the most pernicious of folk-sayings is, 'I could scarcely believe my eyes.' Why should you believe your eyes? You were given eyes to see with, not to believe with. Believe your mind, your intuition, your reason, your feelings if you like—but not your eyes unaided by any of these interpreters. Your eyes can see the mirage, the hallucination, as easily as the actual scenery. Your eyes will tell you nothing exists but matter—"

"Not my eyes only, but my boss."

"Ay? What are you saying?" For all his amiability Enfandin enjoyed interruption in mid-discourse no more than any other teacher. But in a moment his irritation vanished and he listened to my description of Tyss's mechanistic creed.

"God have mercy on his soul," he muttered at last. "Poor creature. He has liberated himself from the superstitions of religion in order to fall into superstition so abject no Christian can conceive it. Imagine to yourself—" he began to pace the floor "—time is circular, man is automaton, we are doomed to repeat the same gestures over and over, forever. Oh I say to you, Hodge, this is monstrous. The poor man. The poor man."

I nodded. "Yes. But what is the answer? Limitless space? Limitless time? They are almost as horrifying, because they are inconceivable and awful."

"And why should the inconceivable and awful be horrifying? Is our small human understanding the ultimate measuring stick and guide? But of course this is not the answer. The answer is that all—time, space, matter—all is illusion. All but the good God Himself. Nothing is real but Him. We are creatures of His fancy, figments of His imagination . . ."

"Then where does free will come in?"

"As a gift, naturally. Or supernaturally. How else? The greatest gift and the greatest responsibility."

I can't say I was entirely satisfied with his exposition, though it was certainly more to my taste than Tyss's. I returned to the conversation at intervals, both in my thoughts and when I saw him, but in the end I suppose all I really accepted was his admonition to be skeptical, which I doubt I always applied the way he meant me to.

7. OF CONFEDERATE AGENTS
   IN 1942

TO ANYONE but the mooncalf I still was in the year of my majority it would have long since occurred with considerable force that Enfandin ought to be told of Tyss's connection with the Negro-hating, anti-foreign Grand Army. And the thought once entertained, no matter how belatedly, would have been immediately translated into warning. For me it became a dilemma.

If I exposed Tyss to Enfandin I would certainly be basely ungrateful to the man who had saved me from destitution and given me the opportunity I wanted so much. Membership in the Grand Army was a crime, even though the laws were laxly enforced, and I could hardly expect an official receiving the hospitality of the United States to conceal knowledge of a felony against his host, especially when the Grand Army was what it was. Yet if I kept silent I would be less than a friend.

If I spoke I would be an informer; if I didnt, a hypocrite and worse. The fact that neither man, for totally different reasons, would condemn me whichever course I took increased rather than diminished my perplexity. I procrastinated, which meant I was actually protecting Tyss, and that this was against my sympathies increased my feeling of guilt.

At this juncture a series of events involved me still deeper with the Grand Army and further complicated my relationship to both Tyss and Enfandin. It began the day a customer called himself to my attention with a selfconscious clearing of his throat.

"Yes sir. Can I help you?"

He was a fat little man with palpably false teeth, and hair hanging down behind over his collar. However the sum of his appearance was in no way ludicrous; rather he gave the impression of ease and authority, and an assurance so strong there was no necessity to buttress it.

"Why, I was looking for—" he began, and then scrutinized me sharply. "Say, aint you the young fella I saw walking with a Nigra? Big black buck?"

Seemingly everyone had been fascinated by the spectacle of two people of slightly different shades of color in company with each other. I felt myself reddening. "There's no law against it, is there?"

He made a gargling noise which I judged was laughter. "Wouldnt know about your damyankee laws, boy. For myself I'd say there's no harm in it, no harm in it at all. Always did like to be around Nigras myself. But then I was rared among em. Most damyankees seem to think Nigras aint fitten company. Only goes to show how narrerminded and bigoted you folks can be. Present company excepted."

"M'sieu Enfandin is consul of the Republic of Haiti," I said; "he's a scholar and a gentleman." As soon as the words were out I was bitterly sorry for their condescension and patronage. I felt ashamed, as if I had betrayed him by offering credentials to justify my friendship and implying it took special qualities to overcome the handicap of his color.

"A mussoo, huh? Furrin and educated Nigra? Well, guess theyre all right." His tone, still hearty, was slightly dubious. "Ben working here long?"

"Nearly four years."

"Kind of dull, aint it?"

"Oh no—I like to read, and there are plenty of books around here."

He frowned. "Should think a hefty young fella'd find more interesting things. Youre indented, of course? No? Well then youre a mighty lucky fella. In a way, in a way. Naturally youll be short on cash, ay? Unless you draw a lucky number in the lottery."

I told him I'd never bought a lottery ticket.

He slapped his leg as though I'd just repeated a very good joke. "Aint that the pattrun," he exclaimed; "aint that the pattrun! Necessity makes em have a lottery; Puritanism keeps em from buying tickets. Aint that the pattrun!" He gargled the humor of it for some time, while his eyes moved restlessly around the dim interior of the store. "And what do you read, ay? Sermons? Books on witches?"

I admitted I'd dipped into both, and then, perhaps trying to impress him, explained my ambitions.

"Going to be a professional historian, hey? Little out of my line, but I don't suppose they's many of em up North here."

"Not unless you count a handful of college instructors who dabble in it."

He shook his head. "Young fella with your aims could do better down South, I'd think."

"Oh yes; some of the most interesting research is going on right now in Leesburg, Washington-Baltimore and the University of Lima. You are a Confederate yourself, sir?"

"Southron, yes sir, I am that, and mighty proud of it. Now look a-here, boy: I'll lay all my cards on the table, face up. Youre a free man and you aint getting any pay here. Now how'd you like to do a little job for me? They's good money in it; and I imagine I'd be able to fix up one of those deals—what do they call em? scholarships—at the University of Leesburg, after."

A scholarship at Leesburg. Where the Department of History was engaged on a monumental project—nothing less than a compilation of all known source material on the War of Southron Independence! It was only with the strongest effort that I refrained from agreeing blindly.

"It sounds fine, Mr—?"

"Colonel Tolliburr. Jest call me cunnel."

There wasnt anything remotely military in his bearing. "It sounds good to me, Colonel. What is the job?"

He clicked his too regular teeth thoughtfully. "Hardly anything at all, m'boy, hardly anything at all. Just want you to keep a list for me."

He seemed to think this a complete explanation. "What kind of list, Colonel?"

"Why, list of the people that come in here steady. Especially the ones don't seem to buy anything, just talk to your boss. Names if you know em, but that aint real important, and a sort of rough description. Like five foot nine, blue eyes, dark hair, busted nose, scar on right eyebrow. And so on. Nothing real detailed. And a list of deliveries."

Was I tempted? I don't really know. "I'm sorry, Colonel. I'm afraid I can't help you."

"Not even for that scholarship and say, a hundred dollars in real money?"

I shook my head.

"They's no harm in it, boy. Likely nothing'll come of it."

"I'm sorry."

"Two hundred? I'm not talking about yankee slugs, but good CSA bills, each with a picture of President Jimmy right slapdash on the middle of it."

"It's not a matter of money, Colonel Tolliburr."

He looked at me shrewdly. "Think it over, boy. No use being hasty." He handed me a card. "Any time you change your mind come and see me or send me a telegram."

I watched him out of the store. The Grand Army must be annoying the mighty Confederacy. Tyss ought to know about the agent's interest. And I knew I would be unable to tell him.

"Suppose," I asked Enfandin the next day, "suppose one were placed in the position of being an involuntary assistant in a—to a . . ."

I was at a loss for words to describe the situation without being incriminatingly specific. I could not tell him about Tolliburr and my clear duty to let Tyss know of the colonel's espionage without revealing Tyss's connection with the Grand Army and thus uncovering my deceit in not warning Enfandin earlier. Whatever I said or failed to say, I was somehow culpable.

He waited patiently while I groped, trying to formulate a question which was no longer a question. "You can't do evil that good may come of it," I burst out at last.

"Quite so. And then?"

"Well . . . That might mean eventually giving up all

action entirely, since we can never be sure even the most innocent act may not have bad consequences."

He nodded. "It might. The Manichaeans thought it did; they believed good and evil balanced and man was created in the image of Satan. But certainly there is a vast difference between this inhuman dogma and refusing to do consciously wicked deeds."

"Maybe," I said dubiously.

He looked at me speculatively. "A man is drowning in the river. I have a rope. If I throw him the rope he may not only climb to safety but take it from me and use it to garrote some honest citizen. Shall I therefore let him drown because I must not do good lest evil come of it?"

"But sometimes they are so mixed up it is impossible to disentangle them."

"Impossible? Or very difficult?"

"Um . . . I don't know."

"Are you not perhaps putting the problem too abstractly? Is not perhaps your situation—your hypothetical situation—one of being accessory to wrong rather than facing an alternative which means personal unhappiness?"

Again I struggled for noncommittal words. He had formulated my dilemma about the Grand Army so far as it connected with giving up my place in the bookstore or telling him of Tyss's bias. Yet not entirely. And why could I not let Tyss know of Colonel Tolliburr's visit, which it was certainly my duty to do? Was this overscrupulousness only a means of avoiding any unpleasantness?

"Yes," I muttered at last.

"It would be very nice if there were no drawbacks ever attached to the virtuous choice. Then the only ones who would elect to do wrong would be those of twisted minds, the perverse, the insane. Who would prefer the devious course if the straight one were just as easy? No, no, my dear Hodge; one cannot escape the responsibility for his choice simply because the other way means inconvenience or hardships or tribulation."

"Must we always act, whether we are sure of the outcome of our action or not?"

"Not acting is also action; can we always be sure of the outcome of refusing to act?"

Was it pettiness that made me contrast his position as an official of a small yet fairly secure power, well enough paid to live comfortably, with mine where a break with Tyss meant beggary and no further chance of fulfilling the ambition every day more important to me? *Did* circumstances alter cases, and was it easy for Enfandin to talk as he did, unconfronted with harsh alternatives?

"You know, Hodge," he said as though changing the subject, "I am what they call a career man, meaning I have no money except my salary. This might seem much to you, but it is really little, particularly since protocol says I must spend more than necessary. For the honor of my country. At home I have an establishment to keep up where my wife and children live—"

I had wondered about his apparent bachelorhood.

"—because to be rudely frank, I do not think they would be happy or safe in the United States on account of their color. Besides these expenses I make personal contributions for the assistance of black men who are—how shall we say it?—unhappily circumstanced in your country, for I have found the official allotment is never enough. Now I have been indiscreet; you know state secrets. Why do I tell you this? Because, my friend, I should like to help. Alas, I cannot offer money. But this I can do, if it will not offend your pride: I suggest you live here—it will be no more uncomfortable than the arrangements you have described in the store—and attend one of the colleges of the city. A medal or an order from the Haitian government judiciously conferred on an eminent educator—decorations cut so nicely across color-lines, perhaps because they don't show their origin to the uninitiated—should take care of tuition fees. What do you say?"

What could I say? That I did not deserve his generosity? The statement would be meaningless, a catchphrase, unless I explained that I'd not been open with him, and now even less than before was I able to do this. Or could I say that bare minutes earlier I had thought enviously and spitefully of him? Wretched and happy, I mumbled incoherent thanks, began a number of sentences and left them unfinished, lapsed into dazed silence.

But the newly opened prospect cut through my introspection and scattered my self-reproaches. The future was too exciting to dwell in any other time; in a moment we were both sketching rapid plans and supplementing each other's designs with revisions of our own. Words tumbled out; ideas were caught in mid-expression. We decided, we reconsidered, we returned to the first decisions.

I was to give Tyss two weeks' notice despite the original agreement making such nicety superfluous; Enfandin was to discuss matriculation with a professor he knew. My employer raised a quizzical eyebrow at my information.

"Ah, Hodgins, you see how neatly the script works out. Nothing left to chance or choice. If you hadnt been relieved of your trifling capital by a man of enterprise whose methods were more successful than subtle you might have fumbled at the edge of the academic world for four years and then, having substituted a wad of unrelated facts for common sense and whatever ability to think you may have possessed, fumbled for the rest of your life at the edge of the economic world. You wouldnt have met George Pondible or gotten here where you could discover your own mind without adjustment to a professorial iron maiden."

"I thought it was all arbitrary."

He gave me a reproachful look. "Arbitrary and predetermined are not synonymous, Hodgins, nor does either rule out artistry. Mindless artistry of course, like that of the snowflake or crystal. And how artistic this development is! You will go on to become a professor yourself and construct iron maidens for promising students who might become your competitors. You will write learned histories, for you are—havent I said this before?—the spectator type. The part written for you does not call for you to be a participant, an instrument for — apparently — influencing events. Hence it is proper that you report them so future generations may get the illusion they arent puppets."

He grinned at me. At another time I would have been delighted to pounce on the assortment of inconsistencies he had just offered; at the moment I could think of nothing but my failure to mention the Confederate agent's visit. It almost seemed his mechanist notions were valid and I was destined always to be the ungrateful recipient of kindness.

"All right," he said, swallowing the last of his bread and half-raw meat; "so long as your sentimentality impels you to respect obligations I can find work for you. Those boxes over there go upstairs. Pondible's bringing a van around for them this afternoon."

Ive heard the assumption that working in a bookstore must be light and pleasant. Many times during the years with Roger Tyss I had reason to be thankful for my strength and farm training. The boxes were deceptively small but so heavy they could only have been solidly packed with paper. Even with Tyss carrying box for box with me I was vastly relieved when I had to quit to run an errand.

When I got back he went out to make an offer on someone's library. "There are only four left. The last two are paper-wrapped; didnt have enough boxes."

It was characteristic of him to leave the lighter packages for me. I ran up the stairs with one of the two remaining wooden containers. Returning, I tripped on the lowest step and sprawled forward. Reflexively I threw out my hands and landed on one of the paper parcels. The tight-stretched covering cracked and split under the impact; the contents —neatly tied rectangular bundles—spilled out.

I had learned enough of the printing trade to recognize the brightly colored oblongs as lithographs, and I wondered as I stooped over to gather them up why such a job should have been given Tyss rather than a shop specializing in this work. Even under the gaslight the colors were hard and vigorous.

Then I really looked at the bundle I was holding. ES-PAÑA was enscrolled across the top; below it was the picture of a man with long nose and jutting underlip, flanked by two ornate figure fives, and beneath them the legend, CINCO PESETAS. Spanish Empire banknotes. Bundles and bundles of them.

I needed neither expert knowledge nor minute scrutiny to tell me there was a fortune here in counterfeit money. The purpose in forging Spanish currency I could not see;

that it was no private undertaking of Tyss's but an activity of the Grand Army I was certain. Puzzled and worried, I rewrapped the bundles of notes into as neat an imitation of the original package as I could contrive.

The rest of the day I spent casting uneasy glances at the mound of boxes and watching with apprehension the movement of anyone toward them. Death was the penalty for counterfeiting United States coins; I had no idea of the punishment for doing the same with foreign paper but I was sure even so minor an accessory as myself would be in a sad way if some officious customer should stumble against one of the packages.

Tyss in no way acted like a guilty man, or even one with an important secret. He seemed unaware of any peril; doubtless he was daily in similar situations, only chance and my own lack of observation had prevented my discovering this earlier.

Nor did he show anxiety when Pondible failed to arrive. Darkness came and the gaslamps went on in the streets. The heavy press of traffic outside dwindled, but the incriminating boxes remained undisturbed near the door. At last there was the sound of uncertain wheels slowing up outside and Pondible's voice admonishing, "Wh-whoa!"

I rushed out just as he was dismounting with slow dignity. "Who goes?" he asked; "Vance and give a countersign."

"It's Hodge," I said. "Let me help you."

"Hodge! Old friend; not seen long time!" (He had been in the store only the day before.) "Terrible sfortune, Hodge. Dri-driving wagon. Fell off. Fell off wagon I mean. See?"

"Sure, I see. Let me hitch the horse for you. Mr Tyss is waiting."

"Avoidable," he muttered, "nuvoidable, voidable. Fell off."

Tyss took him by the arm. "You come with me and rest awhile. Hodgins, you better start loading up; youll have to do the delivering now."

Rebellious refusal formed in my mind. Why should I be still further involved? He had no right to demand it of me; in self-protection I was bound to refuse. "Mr Tyss . . ."

"Yes?"

Two weeks would see me free of him, but nothing could wipe out the debt I owed him. "Nothing. Nothing," I murmured and picked up one of the boxes.

8. IN VIOLENT TIMES

*H*E GAVE ME an address on Twenty-Sixth Street. "Sprovis is the name."

"All right," I said as stolidly as I could.

"Let them do the unloading. I see there's a full feedbag in the van; that'll be a good time to give it to the horse."

"Yes."

"They'll load up another consignment and drive with you to the destination. Take the van back to the livery stable. Here's money for your supper and carfare back here."

He thinks of everything, I reflected bitterly. Except that I don't want to have anything to do with this.

Driving slackly through the almost empty streets my resentment continued to rise, drowning, at least partly, my fear of being for some unfathomable reason stopped by a police officer and apprehended. Why should I be stopped? Why should the Grand Army counterfeit pesetas?

The address, which I had trouble finding on the poorly lit thoroughfare, was one of those four-storey stuccos at least a century old, showing few signs of recent repair. Mr Sprovis, who occupied the basement, had one ear distinctly larger than the other, an anomaly I could not help attributing to a trick of constantly pulling on the lobe. He, like the others who came out with him to unload the van, wore the Grand Army beard.

"I had to come instead of Pon—"

"No names," he growled. "Hear? No names."

"All right. I was told you'd unload and load up again."

"Yeah, yeah."

I slipped the strap of the feedbag over the horse's ear and started toward Eighth Avenue.

"Hey! Where you going?"

"To get something to eat. Anything wrong with that?"

I felt him peering suspiciously at me. "Guess not. But don't keep us waiting, see? We'll be ready to go in twenty minutes."

I did not like Mr Sprovis. In the automatic lunchroom where the dishes were delivered by a clever clockwork device as coins were deposited in the right slots, I gorged on fish and potatoes, but my pleasure at getting away for once from the unvarying bread and heart was spoiled by the thought of him. And I was at best no more than half through with the night's adventure. What freight Sprovis and his companions were now loading in the van I had no idea. Except that it was nothing innocent.

When I turned the corner into Twenty-Sixth Street again, the shadowy mass of the horse and van was gone from its place by the curb. Alarmed, I broke into a run and discovered it turning in the middle of the block. I jumped and caught hold of the dash, pulling myself aboard. "What's the idea?"

A fist caught me in the shoulder, almost knocking me back into the street. Zigzags of shock ran down my arm, terminating in numbing pain. Desperately I clung to the dash.

"Hold it," someone rumbled; "it's the punk who came with. Let him in."

Another voice, evidently belonging to the man who'd hit me, admonished, "Want to watch yourself, chum. Not go jumping like that without warning. I might of stuck a shiv in your ribs instead of my hand."

I could only repeat, "What's the idea of trying to run off with the van? I'm responsible for it."

"He's responsible, see," mocked another voice from the body of the van. "Aint polite not to wait on him."

I was wedged between the driver and my assailant; my shoulder ached and I was beginning to be really frightened now my first anger had passed. These were "action" members of the Grand Army; men who regularly committed battery, mayhem, arson, robbery and murder. I had been both foolhardy and lucky; realizing this it seemed diplomatic not to try for possession of the reins.

I could hear the breathing and mumbling of others in back, but it didnt need this to tell me the van was overloaded. We turned north on Sixth Avenue; the street lights showed Sprovis driving. "Gidap, gidap," he urged, "get going!"

"That's a horse," I protested; "not a locomotive."

"What do you know?" came from behind; "And we thought we was on the Erie."

"He's tired," I persisted, "and he's pulling too much weight."

"Shut up," ordered Sprovis quietly. "Shut up." The quietness was not deceptive; it was ominous. I shut up.

Speed was stupid on several counts. For one thing it called attention to the van at a time when most commercial vehicles had been stabled for the night and the traffic was almost entirely carriages, buggies, hacks and minibiles. I visualized the suspicious crowd which would gather immediately if our horse dropped from exhaustion. There was no hope that consciousness of an innocuous cargo made Sprovis bold; whatever we carried was bound to be as incriminating as the counterfeit bills.

Disconnected scraps of conversation drifted from Sprovis' companions. "I says, 'Look here, youre making a nice profit from selling abroad. Either you . . .'"

"And of course he put it all on a twenty-dollar ticket even though . . ."

"'. . . my taxes,' he says. 'You worry about your taxes,' I says; 'I'm worried about your contributions.'"

A monotonous chuffing close behind us forced itself into my consciousness; when we turned eastward in the Forties I exclaimed, "There's a minibile following us!"

Even as I spoke the trackless engine pulled alongside and then darted ahead to pocket us by nosing diagonally toward the curb. The horse must have been too weak to shy; he simply stopped short and I heard the curses of the felled passengers behind me.

"Not the cops anyway!"

"Cons for a nickel!"

"Only half a block from—"

"Quick, break out the guns—"

"Not those guns; one bang and we're through. Air pistols, if anybody's got one. Hands or knives. Get them all!"

They piled out swiftly past me; I remained alone on the seat, an audience of one, properly ensconced. A few blocks away was the small park where Tirzah used to meet me. It was not believable that this was happening in one of New York's quietest residential districts in the year 1942.

An uneven, distorting light emphasized the abnormal speed of the incident that followed, making the action seem jumpy, as though the participants were caught at static moments, changing their attitudes between flashes of visibility. The tempo was so swift any possible spectators in the bordering windows or on the sidewalks wouldnt have had time to realize what was going on before it was all over.

Four men from the minibile were met by five from the van. The odds were not too unequal, for the attackers had a discipline which Sprovis' force lacked. Their leader attempted to parley during one of those seconds of apparent inaction. "Hay you men—we got nothing against you. They's a thousand dollars apiece in it for you—"

A fist smacked into his mouth. The light caught his face as he was jolted back, but I hardly needed its revelation to confirm my recognition of Colonel Tolliburr's voice.

The Confederate agents had brass knuckles and blackjacks, Colonel Tolliburr had a sword-cane which he unsheathed with a glinting flourish. The Grand Army men flashed knives; no one seemed to be using air pistols or spring-powered guns.

Both sides were intent on keeping the clash as quiet and inconspicuous as possible; no one shouted with anger or screamed in pain. This muffled intensity made the struggle more gruesome; the contenders fought their natural impulses as well as each other. I heard the impact of blows, the grunts of effort, the choked-back cries, the scraping of shoes on pavement and the thud of falls. One of the defenders fell, and two of the attackers, before the two remaining Southrons gave up the battle and attempted escape.

With united impulse they started for the minibile, evidently realized they wouldnt have time to get up power, and began running down the street. Their moment of indecision did for them. As the four Grand Army men closed in I saw the Confederates raise their arms in the traditional gesture of surrender. Then they were struck down.

I crept noiselessly down on the off-side of the van and hastened quietly away in the protection of the shadows.

9. BARBARA

*F*OR THE NEXT few days reading was pure pretense.
I used the opened book to mask my privacy while I
trembled not so much with fear as with horror. I had been
brought up in a harsh enough world and murder was no
novelty in New York; I had seen slain men before, but this
was the first time I had been confronted with naked, merci-
less savagery. Though I believed Sprovis would have had
no qualms about despatching an inconvenient witness if I
had stayed on the van, I had no particular fear for my
own safety, for my knowledge of what had happened became less dangerous daily. The terror of the deed itself
however remained constant.

I was not concerned solely with revulsion. Inquisitive-
ness looked out under loathing to make me wonder what
lay behind the night's events. What had really happened,
and what did it all mean?

From scraps of conversation accidentally heard or deliberately eavesdropped, from the newspapers, from deduction and remembered fragments, I reconstructed the picture which made the background. Its borders reached a
long way from Astor Place.

For years the world had been waiting, half in dread,
half in resignation, for war to break out between the world's
two Great Powers, the German Union and the Confederate
States. Some expected the point of explosion would be the
Confederacy's ally, the British Empire; most anticipated at
least part of the war would be fought in the United States.

The scheme of the Grand Army, or of that part of it

which included Tyss, was apparently a farfetched and fantastic attempt to circumvent the probable course of history. The counterfeiting was an aspect of this attempt which was nothing less than trying to force the war to start, not through the Confederacy's ally, but through the German Union's—the Spanish Empire. With enormous amounts of the spurious currency circulated by emissaries posing as Confederate agents, the Grand Army hoped to embroil the Confederacy with Spain and possibly preserve the neutrality of the United States. It was an ingenuous idea evolved, I see now, by men without knowledge of the actual mechanics of world politics.

If I ever had any sentimental notions about the Army they vanished now. Tyss's mechanism may not have been purposefully designed to palliate, but it made it easy to justify actions like Sprovis'. I had no such convenient way of numbing my conscience. But even as I brooded over the weakness and cowardice which made me an accomplice, I looked forward to my release. I had not seen Enfandin since his offer; in a week I would leave the bookstore for his sanctuary, and I resolved my first act should be to tell him everything. And then that dream was exploded just as it was about to be realized.

I do not know who it was broke into the consulate or for what reason, and was surprised in the act, shooting and wounding Enfandin so seriously he was unable to speak for the weeks before he was finally returned to Haiti to recuperate or die. He could not have gotten in touch with me and I was not permitted to see him; the police guard was doubly zealous to keep him from all contact since he was both an accredited diplomat and a black man.

I did not know who shot him. It was most unlikely to be anyone connected with the Grand Army, but I did not know. I could not know. He *might* have been shot by Sprovis or George Pondible. Since the ultimate chain could have led back to me, it did lead back to me. If this were the Manichaeism of which Enfandin had spoken, I could not help it.

The loss of my chance to escape from the bookstore was the least of my despair. It seemed to me I was caught by the inexorable, choiceless circumstance in which Tyss so firmly believed and Enfandin denied. I could escape neither my guilt nor the surroundings conducive to further guilt. I could not change destiny.

Was all this merely the self-torture of any introverted young man? Possibly. I only know that for a long time, long as one in his early twenties measures time, I lost all interest in life, even dallying with thoughts of suicide. I put books aside distastefully or, which was worse, indifferently.

I must have done my work around the store; certainly I recall no comments from Tyss about it. Neither can I remember anything to distinguish the succession of days. Obviously I ate and slept; there were undoubtedly long hours free from utter hopelessness. The details of those months have simply vanished.

Nor can I say precisely when it was my despair began to lift. I know that one day—it was cold and the snow was deep on the ground, deep enough to keep the minibiles off the streets and cause the horse-cars trouble—I saw a girl walking briskly, red-cheeked, breathing in quick visible puffs, and my glance was not apathetic. When I returned to the bookstore I picked up Field Marshal Liddell-Hart's *Life of General Pickett* and opened it to the place where I had abandoned it. In a moment I was fully absorbed.

Paradoxically, once I was myself again I was no longer the same Hodge Backmaker. For the first time I was determined to do what I wanted instead of waiting and hoping events would somehow turn out right for me. Somehow I was going to free myself from the bookstore and all its frustrations and evils.

This resolution was reinforced by the discovery that I was exhausting the volumes around me. The books I sought now were rare and ever more difficult to find. Innocent of knowledge about academic life I imagined them ready to hand in any college library.

Nor was I any longer satisfied with the printed word alone. My friendship with Enfandin had shown me how fruitful a personal, face-to-face relationship between teacher and student could be, and it seemed to me such ties could develop into ones between fellow scholars, a mutual, uncompetitive pursuit of knowledge.

Additionally I wanted to search the real, the original sources: unpublished manuscripts of participants or onlookers, old diaries and letters, wills or accountbooks, which might shade a meaning or subtly change the interpretation of old, forgotten actions.

My problems could be solved ideally by an instructorship at some college, but how was this to be achieved without the patronage of a Tolliburr or an Enfandin? I had no credentials worth a second's consideration. Though the immigration bars kept out graduates of foreign universities, no college in the United States would accept a self-taught young man who had not only little Latin and less Greek, but no mathematics, languages, or sciences at all. For a long time I considered possible ways and means, both drab and dramatic; at last, more in a spirit of whimsical absurdity than sober hope, I wrote out a letter of application, setting forth the qualifications I imagined myself to possess, assaying the extent of my learning with a generosity only ingenuousness could palliate, and outlining the work I projected for my future. With much care and many revisions I set this composition in type. It was undoubtedly a foolish gesture, but not having access to so costly a machine as a typewriter, and not wanting to reveal this by penning the letters by hand, I resorted to this transparent device.

Tyss picked up one of the copies I struck off and glanced over it. His expression was critical. "Is it too bad?" I asked despondently.

"You should have used more leading. And lined it up and justified the lines and eliminated hyphens. Setting type can never be done mechanically or half-heartedly—that's why no one yet has been able to invent a practical typesetting machine. I'm afraid you'll never make a passable printer, Hodgins."

He was concerned only with typesetting, uninterested in the outcome. Or satisfied, since it was predetermined, that comment was superfluous.

Government mails, never efficient and always expensive,

being one of the favorite victims of holdup men, and pneumatic post limited to local areas, I dispatched the letters
by Wells, Fargo to a comprehensive list of colleges. I can't
say I then waited for the replies to flow in, for though I
knew the company's system of heavily armed guards would
insure delivery of my applications, I had little anticipation
of any answers. As a matter of fact I put it pretty well out
of my mind, dredging it up at rarer intervals, always a trifle
more embarrassed by my presumption.

It was several months later, toward the end of Septem-
ber, that the telegram came signed Thomas K Haggerwells.
It read, ACCEPT NO OFFER TILL OUR REPRESENTATIVE
EXPLAINS HAGGERSHAVEN.

I hadnt sent a copy of my letter to York, Pennsylvania,
where the telegram had originated, or anywhere near it. I
knew of no colleges in that vicinity. And I had never heard
of Mr (or Doctor or Professor) Haggerwells. I might have
thought the message a mean joke, except that Tyss's nature
didnt run to such humor and no one else knew of the letters
except those to whom they were addressed.

I found no reference to Haggershaven in any of the di-
rectories I consulted, which wasnt too surprising consider-
ing the slovenly way these were put together. I decided that
if such a place existed I could only wait patiently until the
"representative," if there really was one, arrived.

Tyss having left for the day, I swept a little, dusted some,
straightened a few of the books—any serious attempt to
arrange the stock would have been futile—and took up a
recent emendation of Creasy's *Fifteen Decisive Battles* by
one Captain Eisenhower.

I was so deep in the good captain's analysis (he might
have made a respectable strategist himself, given an opportunity) that I heard no customer enter, sensed no impatient
presence. I was only recalled from my book by a rather
sharp, "Is the proprietor in?"

"No maam," I answered, reluctantly abandoning the
page. "He's out for the moment. Can I help you?"

My eyes, accustomed to the store's poor light, had the
advantage over hers, still adjusting from the sunlit street.
Secure in my audacity, I measured her vital femininity, a

quality which seemed, if such a thing is possible, imper-
sonal. There was nothing overtly bold or provocative about
her, though I'm sure my mother would have thinned her
lips at the black silk trousers and the jacket which emphasized the contour of her breasts. At a time when women
used every device to call attention to their helplessness and
consequently their desirability and the implied need for
men to protect them, she carried an air which seemed to
say, Why yes, I am a woman: not furtively or brazenly or
incidentally but primarily; what are you going to do about
it?

I recognized a sturdy sensuality as I recognized the fact
that she was bareheaded, almost as tall as I, and rather
large-boned; certainly there was nothing related to me
about it. Nor was it connected with surface attributes; she
was not beautiful and still further from being pretty, though
she might have been called handsome in a way. Her hair,
ginger-colored and clubbed low on her neck, waved crisply;
her eyes appeared slate gray. (Later I learned they could
vary from pale gray to blue-green.) The fleshly greediness
was betrayed, if at all, only by the width and set of her
lips, and that insolent expression.

She smiled, and I decided I had been quite wrong in
thinking her tone peremptory. "I'm Barbara Haggerwells.
I'm looking for a Mr Backmaker"—she glanced at a slip
of paper—"a Hodgins M Backmaker who evidently uses
this as an accommodation address."

"I'm Hodge Backmaker," I muttered in despair. "I—I
work here." I was conscious of not having shaved that
morning, that my pants and jacket did not match, that my
shirt was not clean.

I suppose I expected her to say nastily, So I see! or the
usual, It must be fascinating! Instead she said, "I wonder
if youve run across *The Properties of X* by Whitehead? Ive
been trying to get a copy for a long time."

"Uh—I . . . Is it a mystery story?"

"I'm afraid not. It's a book on mathematics by a mathematician very much out of favor. It's hard to find, I suppose because the author is bolder than he is tactful."

So naturally and easily she led me away from my embarrassment and into talking of books, relieving me of self-consciousness and some of the mortification in being exposed at my humble job by the "representative" of the telegram. I admitted deficient knowledge of mathematics and ignorance of Mr Whitehead though I maintained, accurately, that the book was not in stock, while she assured me that only a specialist would have heard of so obscure a theoretician. This made me ask, with the awe one feels for an expert in an alien field, if she were a mathematician, to which she replied, "Heavens, no. I'm a physicist. But mathematics is my tool."

I looked at her with respect. Anyone, I thought, can read a few books and set himself up as an historian; to be a physicist means genuine learning. And I doubted she was much older than I.

She said abruptly, "My father is interested in knowing something about you."

I acknowledged this with something between a nod and a bow. She had been examining and gauging me for the past half hour. "Your father is Thomas Haggerwells?"

"Haggerwells of Haggershaven," she confirmed, as though explaining everything. There was pride in her voice and a hint of superciliousness.

"I'm dreadfully sorry, Miss Haggerwells, but I'm afraid I'm as ignorant of Haggershaven as of mathematics."

"I thought you said you'd been reading history. Odd youve come upon no reference to the Haven in the records of the past seventy-five years."

I shook my head helplessly. "I suppose my reading has been scattered." Her look indicated agreement but not absolution. "Haggershaven is a college?"

"No. Haggershaven is . . . Haggershaven." She resumed her equanimity, her air of smiling tolerance. "It's hardly a college since it has no student body nor faculty. Rather, both are one at the haven. Anyone admitted is a scholar or potential scholar anxious to devote himself to learning. I mean for its own sake. Not many are acceptable."

She need hardly have added this; it seemed obvious I could not be one of the elect, even if I hadnt offended her by never having heard of Haggershaven. I knew I couldnt pass the most lenient of entrance examinations to ordinary colleges, much less to the dedicated place she represented.

"There arent any formal requirements for fellowship," she went on, "beyond the undertaking to work to full capacity, to pool all knowledge and hold back none from scholars anywhere, to contribute economically to the Haven in accordance with decisions of the majority of fellows, and to vote on questions without consideration of personal gain. There! That certainly sounds like the stuffiest manifesto delivered this year."

"It sounds too good to be true."

"Oh, it's true enough." She moved close and I caught the scent of her hair and skin. "But there's another side. The haven is neither wealthy nor endowed. We have to earn our living. The fellows draw no stipend; they have food, clothes, shelter, whatever books and materials they need —no unessentials. We often have to leave our own individual work to do manual labor to bring in food or money for all."

"Ive read of such communities," I said enthusiastically. "I thought they'd all disappeared fifty or sixty years ago."

"Have you and did you?" she asked contemptuously. "Youll be surprised to learn that Haggershaven is neither Owenite nor Fourierist. We are not fanatics nor saviors. We don't live in phalansteries, practice group marriage or vegetarianism. Our organization is expedient, subject to revision, not doctrinaire. Contribution to the common stock is voluntary and we are not concerned with each other's private lives."

"I beg your pardon, Miss Haggerwells. I didnt mean to annoy you."

"It's all right. Perhaps I'm touchy; all my life Ive seen the squinty suspiciousness of the farmers all around, sure we were up to something immoral, or at least illegal. Youve no idea what a prickly armor you build around yourself when you know that every yokel is cackling, 'There goes one of them; I bet they . . .' whatever unconventional practice their imaginations can conceive at the moment. And the parallel distrust of the respectable schools. Detachedly, the haven may indeed be a refuge for misfits, but is it necessarily wrong not to fit into the civilization around us?"

"I'm prejudiced. I certainly havent fitted in myself."

She didnt answer and I felt I had gone too far in daring an impulsive identification. Awkwardness made me blurt out further, "Do you . . . do you think there's any chance Haggershaven would accept me?" Whatever reserve I'd tried to maintain deserted me; my voice expressed only childish longing.

"I couldnt say," she answered primly. "Acceptance or rejection depends entirely on the vote of the whole fellowship. All I'm here to offer is train fare. Neither you nor the haven is bound."

"I'm perfectly willing to be bound," I said fervently.

"You may not be so rash after a few weeks."

I was about to reply when Little Aggie—so called to distinguish her from Fat Aggie who was in much the same trade, but more successful—came in. Little Aggie supplemented her nocturnal earnings around Astor Place by begging in the same neighborhood during the day.

"Sorry, Aggie," I said; "Mr Tyss didnt leave anything for you."

"Maybe the lady would help a poor working girl down on her luck," she suggested, coming close. "My, that's a pretty outfit you have. Looks like real silk, too."

Barbara Haggerwells drew away with anger and loathing on her face. "No," she refused sharply. "No, nothing!" She turned to me. "I must be going. I'll leave you to entertain your friend."

"Oh, I'll go," said Little Aggie cheerfully, "no need to get in an uproar. Bye-bye."

I was frankly puzzled; the puritanical reaction didnt seem consistent. I would have expected condescending amusement, disdainful tolerance or even haughty annoyance, but not this furious aversion. "I'm sorry Little Aggie bothered you. She's really not a wicked character and she does have a hard time getting along."

"I'm sure you must enjoy her company immensely. I'm sorry we can't offer similar attractions at the haven."

Apparently she thought my relations with Aggie were professional. Even so her attitude was odd. I could hardly flatter myself she was interested in me as a man, yet her flare-up seemed to indicate jealousy, a strange kind of jealousy, perhaps like the sensuality I attributed to her, as though the mere presence of another woman was an affront.

"Please don't go yet. For one thing—" I cast around for something to hold her till I could restore a more favorable impression. "—for one thing you havent told me how Haggershaven happened to get my application."

She gave me a cold, angry look. "Even though we're supposed to be cranks, orthodox educators often turn such letters over to us. After all, they may want to apply themselves someday."

The picture this suddenly presented, of a serene academic life which was not so serene and secure after all, but prepared for a way to escape if necessary, was startling to me. I had taken it for granted that our colleges, even though they were far inferior to those of other countries, were stable and sheltered.

When I expressed something of this, she laughed. "Hardly. The colleges have not only decayed, they have decayed faster than other institutions. They are mere hollow shells, ruined ornaments of the past. Instructors spy on each other to curry favor with the trustees and assure themselves of reappointment when the faculty is out periodically. Loyalty is the touchstone, but no one knows any more what the object of loyalty is supposed to be. Certainly it is no longer toward learning, for that is the least of their concerns."

She slowly allowed herself to be coaxed back into her previous mood, and again we talked of books. And now I thought there was a new warmth in her voice and glance, as though she had won some kind of victory, but how or over whom there was no indication.

When she left I hoped she was not too prejudiced against me. For myself I readily admitted it would be easy enough to want her—if one were not afraid of the humiliations it was in her nature to inflict.

10. THE HOLDUP

*T*HIS TIME I didnt offer Tyss two weeks' notice. "Well Hodgins, I made all the appropriate valedictory remarks on a previous occasion, so I'll not repeat them, except to say the precision of the script is extraordinary."

It seemed to me he was saying in a roundabout way that everything was for the best. For the first time I saw Tyss as slightly pathetic rather than sinister; extreme pessimism and vulgar optimism evidently met, like his circular time. I smiled indulgently and thanked him sincerely for all his kindness.

In 1944 almost a hundred years had passed since New York and eastern Pennsylvania were first linked in a railroad network, yet I don't suppose my journey differed much in speed or comfort from one which might have been taken by Granpa Hodgins' father. The steam ferry carried me across the Hudson to Jersey. I had heard there were only financial, not technical obstacles to a bridge or tunnel. If the English and French could burrow under the Channel, as they had early in the century, and the Japanese complete their great tube beneath the Korea Strait, it was hard to see why a lesser work here was dismissed as the impractical suggestion of dreamers who believed the cost would be saved in a few years by running trains directly to Manhattan.

Nor was the ferry the only antique survival on the trip. The cars were all ancient, obvious discards from Confederate or British American lines. Flat wheels were common; the wornout locomotives dragged them protestingly over

86

the wobbly rails and uneven roadbed. First class passengers sat on napless plush or grease-glazed straw seats; second class passengers stood in the aisles or on the platforms; third class rode the roofs—safe enough at the low speed except for sudden jerks or jolts.

There were so many different lines, each jealous of exclusive rights of way, that the traveler hardly got used to his particular car before he had to snatch up his baggage and hustle for the connecting train, which might be on the same track or at the same sooty depot, but was more likely to be a mile away. Even the adjective "connecting" was often ironical for it was not unusual to find time-tables arranged so a departure preceded an arrival by minutes, necessitating a stopover of anywhere from one hour to twelve.

If anything could have quieted my excitement on the trip it was the view through the dirt-sprayed windows. "Fruitless" and "unfulfilled" were the words coming oftenest to my mind. I had forgotten during the past six years just how desolate villages and towns could look when their jerrybuilt structures were sunk in apathetic age without even the false rejuvenation of newer jerrybuilding. I had forgotten the mildewed appearance of tenant farmhouses, the unconvincing attempt to appear businesslike of false-fronted stores with clutters of hopeless merchandise in their dim windows, or the inadequate bluff of factories too small for any satisfactory production.

Once away from New York it was clear how atypical the city was in its air of activity and usefulness. The countryside through which the tracks ran, between fields and pastures or down the center of main streets, should have been the industrial heart of a country bustling and vigorous. Instead one saw potentialities denied, projects withered, poverty and dilapidation.

We crossed the Susquehanna on an old, old stone bridge that made one think of Meade's valiant men, bloodily bandaged many of them, somnambulistically marching northward, helpless and hopeless after the Confederate triumph at Gettysburg, their only thought to escape Jeb Stuart's pursuing cavalry. Indeed, every square mile now carried on its surface an almost visible weight of historical memories.

York seemed old, gray and crabbed in the afternoon, but when I got off the train there I was too agitated with the prospect of being soon at Haggershaven to take any strong impression of the town. I inquired the way, and the surly response confirmed Barbara Haggerwells' statement of local animosity. The distance, if my informant was accurate, was a matter of some ten miles.

I started off down the highway, building and demolishing daydreams, thinking of Tyss and Tirzah, Enfandin and Miss Haggerwells, trying to picture her father and the fellows of the haven and for the thousandth time marshaling arguments for my acceptance in the face of scornful scrutiny. The early October sun was setting on the rich red and yellow leaves of the maples and oaks; I knew the air would become chilly before long, but exertion kept me warm. I counted on arriving at the haven in plenty of time to introduce myself before bedtime.

Less than a mile out of town the highway assumed the familiar aspect of the roads around Wappinger Falls and Poughkeepsie: rutted, wavering, with deep, unexpected holes. The stone or rail fences on either side enclosed harvested cornfields, the broken stalks a dull brass with copper-colored pumpkins scattered through them. But the fences were in poor repair and the oft-mended wooden covered bridges over the creeks all had signs, DANGEROUS, Travel At Your Own Risk.

There were few to share the highway with me: a farmer with an empty wagon, urging his team on and giving me a churlish glance instead of an invitation to ride; a horseman on an elegant chestnut picking his course carefully among the chuckholes, and a few tramps, each bent on his solitary way, at once defensive and aggressive. The condition of the bridges accounted for the absence of minibiles. However, just about twilight a closed carriage, complete with coachman and footman on the box, rolled haughtily by, stood for a moment outlined atop the slope up which I was trudging and then disappeared down the other side.

I paid little attention except—remembering my boyhood

and my father's smithy—to visualize automatically the coachman pulling back on the reins and the footman thrusting forward with the brake as they eased the horses downward. So when I heard first a shout and then feminine screams my instant conclusion was that the carriage had overturned on the treacherous downgrade, broken an axle, or otherwise suffered calamity.

My responsive burst of speed had almost carried me to the top when I heard the shots. First one, like the barking of an uncertain dog, followed by a volley, as though the pack were unleashed.

I ran to the side of the road, close to the field, where I could see with less chance of being seen. Already the dusk was playing tricks, distorting the shape of some objects and momentarily hiding others. It could not however falsify the scene in the gully below. Four men on horseback covered the carriage with drawn revolvers; a fifth, pistol also in hand, had dismounted. His horse, reins hanging down, was peacefully investigating the roadside weeds.

None of them attempted to stop the terrified rearing of the carriage team. Only their position, strung across the road, prevented a runaway. I could not see the footman, but the coachman, one hand still clutching the reins, was sprawled backward with his foot caught against the dashboard and his head hanging down over the wheel.

The door on the far side was swung open. I thought for a moment the passengers had managed to escape. However as the unmounted highwayman advanced, waving his pistol, the other door opened and a man and two women descended into the roadway. Slowly edging forward I could now plainly hear the gang's obscene whistles at sight of the women.

"Well boys, here's something to warm up a cold night. Hang on to them while I see what the mister has in his pockets."

The gentleman stepped in front, and with a slight accent said, "Take the girl by all means. She is but a peasant, a servant, and may afford you amusement. But the lady is my wife; I will pay you a good ransom for her and myself.

I am Don Jaime Escobar y Gallegos, attached to the Spanish legation."

One of the men on horseback said, "Well now, that's real kind of you, Don High-me. We might have taken you up on that, was you an American. But we can't afford no company of Spanish Marines coming looking for us, so I guess we'll have to pass up the ransom and settle for whatever youve got handy. And Missus Don and the hired girl. Don't worry about her being a peasant; we'll treat her and the madam exactly the same."

"Madre de Dios," screamed the lady. "Mercy!"

"It will be a good ransom," said the Spaniard, "and I give you my word my government will not bother you."

"Sorry, chum," returned the gangster. "You foreigners have a nasty habit of interfering with our domestic institutions and hanging men who make a living this way. Just can't trust you."

The man on foot took a step forward. The nearest rider swung the maid up before him and another horseman reached for her mistress. Again she screamed; her husband brushed the hand aside and put his wife behind him. At that the gangster raised his pistol and shot twice. The man and woman dropped to the ground. The maid shrieked till her captor covered her mouth.

"Now what did you want to do that for? Cutting our woman supply in half that way?"

"Sorry. Mighty damn sorry. These things always happen to me."

Meanwhile another of the gang slid off his horse and the two went through the dead, stripping them of jewelry and whatever articles of clothing caught their fancy before searching the luggage and the coach itself for valuables. By the time they had finished it was fully dark and I had crept to within a few feet of them, crouching reasonably secure and practically invisible while they debated what to do with the horses. One faction was in favor of taking them along for spare mounts; the other, arguing that they were too easily identifiable, for cutting them out and turning them loose. The second group prevailing, they at last galloped away.

A sudden thrashing in the cornstalks just beyond the fence startled me into rigidity. Something which might be human stumbled and crawled toward the carriage, snuffling and moaning, to throw itself down by the prostrate bodies, its anguished noises growing more high-pitched and chilling.

I was certain this must be a passenger who had jumped from the offside of the carriage at the start of the holdup, but whether man or woman it was impossible to tell. I moved forward gingerly, but somehow I must have betrayed my presence, for the creature, with a terrified groan, slumped inertly.

My hands told me it was a woman I raised from the ground and the smell of her was the smell of a young girl. "Don't be afraid, Miss," I tried to reassure her; "I'm a friend."

I could hardly leave the girl lying in the road, nor did I feel equal to carrying her to Haggershaven which I reckoned must be about six miles further. I tried shaking her, rubbing her hands, murmuring encouragement, all the while wishing the moon would come up, feeling somehow it would be easier to revive her in the moonlight.

"Miss," I urged, "get up. You can't stay here—they may come back."

Had I reached her? She stirred, whimpering with strange, muffled sounds. I dragged her to her knees and managed to get her arm over my shoulder. "Get up," I repeated. "Get on your feet."

She moaned. I pulled her upright and adjusted my hold. Supporting her around the waist and impeded by my valise, I began an ungraceful, shuffling march. I could only guess at how much time had been taken up by the holdup and how slow our progress would be. It didnt seem likely we could get to Haggershaven before midnight, an awkward hour to explain the company of a strange girl. The possibility of leaving her at a hospitable farmhouse was remote; no isolated rural family in times like these would open their door with anything but deep suspicion or a shotgun blast.

We had made perhaps a mile, a slow and arduous one,

when the moon rose at last. It was full and bright, and showed my companion to be even younger than I had thought. The light fell on masses of curling hair, wildly disarrayed about a face unnaturally pale and lifeless yet extraordinarily beautiful. Her eyes were closed in a sort of troubled sleep, and she continued to moan, though at less frequent intervals.

I had just decided to stop for a moment's rest when we came upon one of the horses. The clumsily cut traces trailing behind him had caught on the stump of a broken sapling. Though still trembling he was over the worst of his fright; after patting and soothing him I got us onto his back and we proceeded in more comfortable if still not too dignified fashion.

It wasnt hard to find Haggershaven: the sideroad to it was well kept and far smoother than the highway. We passed between what looked to be freshly plowed fields and came to a fair sized group of buildings, in some of which I was pleased to see lighted windows. The girl had still not spoken; her eyes remained closed and she moaned occasionally.

Dogs warned of our approach. From a dark doorway a figure came forward with a rifle under his arm. "Who is it?"

"Hodge Backmaker. Ive got a girl here who was in a holdup. She's had a bad shock."

"All right," he said, "let me hitch the horse. Then I'll help you with the girl. My name's Dorn. Asa Dorn."

I slid off and lifted the girl down. "I couldnt leave her in the road," I offered in inane apology.

"I'll water and feed the horse after. Let's go into the main kitchen; it's warm there. Here," he addressed the girl, "take my arm."

She made no response and I half carried her, with Dorn trying helpfully to share her weight. The building through which we led her was obviously an old farmhouse, enlarged and remodelled a number of times. Gaslights of a strange pattern, brighter than any I'd ever seen, revealed Asa Dorn as perhaps thirty with very broad shoulders and very long arms, and a dark, rather melancholy face. "There's a gang been operating around here," he informed me; "tried to shake the haven down for a contribution. That's why I was on guard with the gun. Must be the same bunch."

We bustled our charge into a chair before a big fieldstone fireplace which gave the large room its look of welcome, though the even heat came from sets of steampipes under the windows. "Should we give her some soup? Or tea? Or shall I get Barbara or one of the other women?"

His fluttering brushed the outside of my mind. Here in the light I instinctively expected to see some faint color in the girl's cheeks or hands, but there was none. She looked no more than sixteen, perhaps because she was severely dressed in some school uniform. Her hair, which had merely been a disordered frame for her face in the moonlight, now showed itself as deeply black, hanging in thick, soft curls around her shoulders. Her features, which seemed made to reflect emotions—full, mobile lips, faintly slanted eyes, high nostrils—were instead impassive, devoid of vitality, and this unnatural quiescence was heightened by the dark eyes, now wide open and expressionless. Her mouth moved slowly, as though to form words, but nothing came forth except the faintest of guttural sounds.

"She's trying to say something." I leaned forward as though by sympathetic magic to help the muscles which seemed to respond with such difficulty.

"Why," exlaimed Dorn, "she's . . . dumb!"

She looked agonizedly toward him. I patted her arm helplessly.

"I'll go get—" he began.

A door opened and Barbara Haggerwells blinked at us. "I thought I heard someone ride up, Ace. Do you suppose . . ." Then she caught sight of the girl. Her face set in those lines of strange anger I had seen in the bookstore.

"Miss Haggerwells—"

"Barbara—"

Dorn and I spoke together. Either she did not hear us or we made no impression. She faced me in offended outrage. "Really, Mr Backmaker, I thought I'd explained there were no facilities here for this sort of thing."

"You misunderstand," I said, "I happened—"

Dorn broke in. "Barbara, she's been in a holdup. She's dumb . . ."

Fury made her ugly. "Is that an additional attraction?"

"Miss Haggerwells," I tried again, "you don't understand—"

"I think I understand very well. Dumb or not, get the slut out of here! Get her out right now, I say!"

"Barbara, youre not listening—"

She continued to face me, her back to him. "I should have remembered you were a ladies' man, Mr Self-taught Backmaker. No doubt you imagined Haggershaven to be some obscene liberty hall. Well, it isnt! You'd be wasting any further time you spent here. Get out!"

11. OF HAGGERSHAVEN

9 SUPPOSE—recalling the inexplicable scene with Little Aggie—I was less astonished by her frenzy than I might have been. Besides, her rage and misunderstanding were anticlimactic after the succession of excitements I had been through that day. Instead of amazement I felt only uneasiness and tired annoyance.

Dorn steered Barbara out of the room with a combination of persuasion and gentle force disguised as solicitous soothing, leaving the girl and me alone. "Well," I said, "well . . ."

The large eyes regarded me helplessly.

"Well, youve certainly caused me a lot of trouble . . ."

Dorn returned with two women, one middleaged, the other slightly younger, who flowed around the girl like soapy water, effectually sealing her away from all further masculine blunders, uttering little bubbly clucks and sudsy comfortings.

"Overwork, Backmaker," Dorn mumbled. "Barbara's been overworking terribly. You mustnt think—"

"I don't," I said. "I'm just sorry she couldnt be made to realize what actually happened."

"Hypersensitive; things that wouldnt ordinarily . . . it's overwork. Youve no idea. She wears herself out. Practically no nerves left."

His face, pleading for understanding, looked even more melancholy than before. I felt sorry for him and slightly superior; at the moment at least I didnt have to apologize for any female unpredictability. "OK, OK; there doesnt

95

seem to be any great harm done. And the girl appears to be in good hands now."

"Oh she is," he answered with evident relief at dropping the subject of Barbara's behavior. "I don't think there's anything more we can do for her now; in fact I'd say we're only in the way. How about meeting Mr Haggerwells now?"

"Why not?" The last episode had doubtless finished me for good so far as Barbara was concerned; whatever neutral report she might have given her father originally could now be counted on for a damning revision. I might as well put a nonchalant face on matters before returning to the world outside Haggershaven.

Thomas Haggerwells, large-boned like his daughter, with the ginger hair faded, and a florid, handsome complexion, made me welcome. "Historian ay, Backmaker? Delighted. Combination of art and science; Clio, most enigmatic of the muses. The ever-changing past, ay?"

"I'm afraid I'm no historian yet, Mr Haggerwells. I'd like to be one. If Haggershaven will let me be part of it."

He patted me on the shoulder. "The fellows will do what they can, Backmaker; you can trust them."

"That's right," said Dorn cheerfully; "you look strong as an ox and historians can be kept happy with books and a few old papers."

"Ace is our cynic," explained Mr Haggerwells; "very useful antidote to some of our soaring spirits." He looked absently around and then said abruptly, "Ace, Barbara is quite upset."

I thought this extreme understatement, but Dorn merely nodded. "Misunderstanding, Mr H."

"So I gathered." He gave a short, selfconscious laugh. "In fact that's all I did gather. She said something about a woman . . ."

"Girl, Mr H, just a girl." He gave a quick outline of what had happened, glossing over Barbara's hysterical welcome.

"I see. Quite an adventure in the best tradition, ay Backmaker? And the victims killed in cold blood; makes you wonder about civilization. Savagery all around us." He began pacing the flowered carpet. "Naturally we must help the poor creature. Shocking, quite shocking. But how can I explain to Barbara? She . . . she came to me," he said half proudly, half apprehensively. "I wouldnt want to fail her; I hardly know . . ." He pulled himself together. "Excuse me, Backmaker. My daughter is highstrung. I fear I'm allowing concern to interfere with our conversation."

"Not at all, sir," I said. "I'm very tired; if you'll excuse me . . ."

"Of course, of course," he answered gratefully. "Ace will show you your room. Sleep well—we'll talk more tomorrow. And Ace—come back here afterward, will you?"

Barbara Haggerwells had both Dorn and her father well cowed, I thought as I lay awake. Clearly she could brook not even the suspicion of rivalry, even when it was entirely imaginary. It would be rather frightening to be her father, or—as I suspected Ace might be—her lover, and subject to her tyrannical dominance.

But it was neither Barbara nor overstimulation from the full day which caused my insomnia. A torment, successfully suppressed for hours, invaded me. Connecting the trip of the Escobars—"attached to the Spanish legation"—with the counterfeit pesetas was pure fantasy. But what is logic? I could not argue myself into reasonableness. I could not quench my feeling of responsibility with ridicule nor convincingly charge myself with perverse conceit in magnifying my trivial errands into accountability for all that flowed from the Grand Army—for much which might have flowed from the Grand Army. Guilty men cannot sleep because they feel guilty. It is the feeling, not the abstract guilt which keeps them awake.

Nor could I pride myself on my chivalry in rescuing distressed maidens. I had only done what was unavoidable, grudgingly, without warmth or charity. There was no point in being aggrieved by Barbara's misinterpretation with its disastrous consequences to my ambitions. I had not freely chosen to help; I had no right to resent a catastrophe which should properly have followed a righteous choice.

At last I slept, only to dream Barbara Haggerwells was a great fish pursuing me over endless roads on which my feet bogged in clinging, tenacious mud. Opening my mouth to shout for help was useless; nothing came forth but a croak which sounded faintly like my mother's favorite "Gumption!"

In the clear autumn morning my notions of the night dwindled, even if they failed to disappear entirely. By the time I was dressed Ace Dorn showed up; we went to the kitchen where Ace introduced me to a middleaged man, Hiro Agati, whose close-cut stiff black hair stood perfectly and symmetrically erect all over his head.

"Dr Agati's a chemist," remarked Ace, "condemned to be head chef for a while on account of being too good a cook."

"Believe that," said Agati, "and you'll believe anything. Truth is they always pick on chemists for hard work. Physicists like Ace never soil their hands. Well, so long as you can't eat with the common folk, what'll you have, eggs or eggs?"

Agati was the first Oriental I'd ever seen. The great anti-Chinese massacres of the 1890's, which generously included Japanese and indeed all with any sign of the epicanthic eyefold, had left few Asians to have descendants in the United States. I'm afraid I stared at him more than was polite, but he was evidently used to such rudeness for he paid no attention.

"They finally got the girl to sleep," Ace informed me. "Had to give her opium. No report yet this morning."

"Oh," I said lamely, conscious I should have asked after her without waiting for him to volunteer the news. "Oh. Do you suppose we'll find out who she is?"

"Mr H telegraphed the sheriff first thing. It'll all depend how interested he is, and that's not likely to be very. What's to drink, Hiro?"

"Imitation tea, made from dried weeds; imitation coffee made from burnt barley. Which'll you have?"

I didnt see why he stressed the imitation; genuine tea and coffee were drunk only by the very rich. Most people preferred "tea" because it was less obnoxious than the counterfeit coffee. Perversely, I said, "Coffee please."

He set a large cup of brown liquid before me which had a tantalizing fragrance quite different from that given off by the beverage I was used to. I added milk and tasted, aware he was watching my reaction.

"Why," I exclaimed, "this is different. I never had anything like it in my life. It's wonderful."

"C eight H ten O two," said Agati with an elaborate air of indifference. "Synthetic. Specialty of the house."

"So chemists are good for something after all," remarked Ace.

"Give us a chance," said Agati; "we could make beef out of wood and silk out of sand."

"Youre a physicist like B—like Miss Haggerwells?" I asked Ace.

"I'm a physicist, but not like Barbara. No one is. She's a genius. A great creative genius."

"Chemists create," said Agati sourly; "physicists sit and think about the universe."

"Like Archimedes," said Ace.

How shall I write of Haggershaven as my eyes first saw it twenty-two years ago? Of the rolling acres of rich plowed land, interrupted here and there by stone outcroppings worn smooth and round by time, and trees in woodlots or standing alone strong and unperturbed? Of the main building, grown by fits and starts from the original farmhouse into a great, rambling eccentricity stopping short of monstrosity only by its complete innocence of pretense? Shall I describe the two dormitories, severely functional, escaping harshness because they had not been built by carpenters and though sturdy enough, betrayed the amateur touch in every line? Or the cottages and apartments, two, four, at most six rooms, for the married fellows and their families? These were scattered all over, some so avid for privacy that one could pass unknowing within feet of the concealing trees or shrubbery, others bold in the sunshine on knolls or in hollows.

I could tell of the small shops, the miniature laboratories, the inadequate observatory, the heterogeneous assortment of books which was both less and more than a library, the dozens of outbuildings. But these things were not the haven. They were merely the least of its possessions. For

Haggershaven was not a material place at all, but a spiritual freedom. Its limits were only the limits of what its fellows could do or think or inquire. It was circumscribed only by the outside world, not by internal rules and taboos, competition or curriculum.

Most of this I could see for myself, much of it was explained by Ace. "But how can you afford the time to take me all around this way?" I asked; "I must be interfering with your own work."

He grinned. "This is my period to be guide, counselor and friend to those whove strayed in here, wittingly or un. Don't worry, after youre a fellow youll get told off for all the jobs, from shoveling manure to gilding weathercocks."

I sighed. "The chances of my getting to be a fellow are minus nothing. Especially after last night."

He didnt pretend to misunderstand. "Barbara'll come out of it. She's not always that way. As her father says, she's high-strung, and she's been working madly. And to tell the truth," he went on in a burst of frankness, "she really doesnt get on too well with other women. She has a masculine mind."

I have often noticed that men not strikingly brilliant themselves attribute masculine minds to intelligent women on the consoling assumption that feminine minds are normally inferior. Ace however was manifestly innocent of any attempt to patronize.

"Anyway," he concluded, "she has only one vote."

I didnt know whether to take this as a pledge of support or mere politeness. "Isnt it wasteful, assigning a chemist like Dr Agati to kitchen work? Or isnt he a good chemist?"

"Just about the best there is. His artificial tea and coffee would bring a fortune to the haven if there were a profitable market; even as it is it'll bring a good piece of change. Wasteful? What would you have us do, hire cooks and servants?"

"Theyre cheap enough."

"Or frightfully expensive. Specialization, the division of labor, is certainly not cheap in anything but dollars and cents, and not always then. And it's unquestionably wasteful in terms of equality. And I don't think there's anyone at the haven who isn't an egalitarian."

"But you do specialize and divide labor. Don't tell me you swap your physics for Agati's chemistry."

"In a way we do. Of course I don't set up as an experimenter, any more than he does as a speculator. But there have been plenty of times Ive worked under his direction when he needed an assistant who didnt know anything but had a strong back."

"All right," I said; "but I still don't see why you can't hire a cook and some dishwashers."

"Where would our equality be then? What would happen to our fellowship?"

Haggershaven's history, which I got little by little, was more than a link with the past; it was a possible hint of what might have been if the War of Southron Independence had not interrupted the American pattern. Barbara's great-great-grandfather, Herbert Haggerwells, had been a Confederate major from North Carolina who, as conquerors sometimes do, had fallen in love with the then fat Pennsylvania countryside. After the war he had put everything —not much by Southron standards, but a fortune in depreciated, soon to be repudiated, United States greenbacks—into the farm which later formed the nucleus of Haggershaven. Then he married a local girl and transformed himself into a Northerner.

Until I became too accustomed to notice it anymore I used to stare at his portrait in the library, picturing in idle fancy a possible meeting on the battlefield between this aristocratic gentleman with his curling mustache and daggerlike imperial and my own plebian Granpa Hodgins. But the chance of their ever having come face to face was much more than doubtful; I, who had studied both their likenesses, was the only link between them.

"Hard looking character, ay?" commented Ace. "This was painted when he was mellow; imagine him twenty years earlier. Pistols cocked and Juvenal or Horace or Seneca in the saddlebags."

"He was a cavalry officer, then?"

"I don't know. Don't think so as a matter of fact. Saddlebags was just my artistic touch. They say he was a holy terror; discipline and all that—it sort of goes with a man on horseback. And the old Roman boys are pure deduction; he was that type. Patronized several writers and artists; you know: 'Drop down to my estate and stay a while' and they stayed five or ten years."

But it was Major Haggerwells' son who, seeing the deterioration of Northern colleges, had invited a few restive scholars to make their home with him. They were free to pursue their studies under an elastic arrangement which permitted them to be selfsupporting through work on the farm.

Thomas Haggerwells' father had organized the scheme further, attracting a larger number of schoolmen who contributed greatly to the material progress of the haven. They patented inventions, marketless at home, which brought regular royalties from more industrialized countries. Agronomists improved the haven's crops and took in a steady income from seed. Chemists found ways of utilizing otherwise wasted byproducts; proceeds from scholarly works—and one more popular than scholarly—added to the funds. In his will, Volney Haggerwells left the properties to the fellowship.

I suppose I expected there would be some uniformity, some basic type characterizing the fellows. Not that Barbara, or Ace, or Hiro Agati resembled a stereotype at any point, any more than I did myself, but then I was not one of the elect nor likely to be. Even after I had met more than half of them the notion persisted that there must be some stamp on them proclaiming what they were.

Yet as I wandered about the haven, alone or with Ace, the people I met were quite diverse, more so by far than in the everyday world. There were the ebullient and the glum, the talkative and the laconic, the bustling and the slow-moving. Some were part of a family, others lived ascetically, withdrawn from the pleasures of the flesh.

In the end I realized there was, if not a similarity, a strong bond. The fellows, conventional or eccentric, passionate or reserved, were all earnest, purposeful and, despite individual variations, tenacious. They were, though

I hesitate to use so emotional a word, dedicated. The cruel struggle and suspicion, the frantic endeavor to improve one's own financial, social, or political standing by maiming or destroying someone else intent on the same endeavor was either unknown or so subdued as to be imperceptible at the haven. Disagreements and jealousies existed, but they were different in kind rather than in degree from those to which I had been accustomed all my life. The pervasive fears which fostered the latter, the same fears which made lotteries and indenture frantic gambles to escape the wretchedness of life, could not circulate in the security of the haven.

After the scene at my arrival, I didnt see Barbara again for some ten days. Even then it was but a glimpse, caught as she hurried in one direction and I sauntered in another. She threw me a single frigid glance and went on. Later, I was talking with Mr Haggerwells, who had proved to be not quite an amateur of history but more than a dabbler, when, without knocking, she burst into the room.

"Father, I—" Then she caught sight of me. "Sorry. I didnt know you were entertaining."

His tone was that of one found in a guilty act. "Come in, come in, Barbara. Backmaker is after all something of a protégé of yours. Urania, you know—if one may stretch the ascription a bit—encouraging Clio."

"Really, Father!" She was regal. Wounded, scornful, but majestic. "I'm sure I don't know enough about self-taught pundits to sponsor them. It seems too bad they have to waste your time—"

He flushed. "Please, Barbara. You must, you really must control . . ."

Her disapproval became open anger. "Must I? Must I? And stand by while every pretentious swindler usurps your attention? Oh, I don't ask for any special favors as your daughter; I know too well I have none coming. But I should think at least the consideration due a fellow of the haven would prompt ordinary courtesy even where no natural affection exists!"

"Barbara, please . . . Oh, my dear girl, how can you . . .?"

But she was gone, leaving him distressed and me puzzled. Not at her lack of restraint but at her accusation that he lacked a father's love for her. Nothing was clearer than his pride in her or his protective, baffled tenderness. It did not seem possible so willful a misunderstanding could be maintained.

"You can't judge Barbara by ordinary standards," insisted Ace uncomfortably, when I told him what had happened.

"I'm not judging her by any standards or at all," I said; "I just don't see how anyone could get things so wrong."

"She . . . Her nature needs sympathy. Lots of it. She's never had the understanding and encouragement she ought to have."

"It looks the other way around to me."

"That's because you don't know the background. She's always been lonely. From childhood. Her mother was impatient of children and never found time for her."

"How do you know?" I asked.

"Why . . . she told me, of course."

"And you believed her. Without corroborative evidence. Is that what's called the scientific attitude?"

He stopped stock-still. "Look here, Backmaker—" a moment before I had been Hodge to him—"Look here, Backmaker, I'm damned tired of all the things people say about Barbara; the jeers and sneers and gossip by people who just aren't good enough to breathe the same air with her, much less have the faintest notion of her mind and spirit—"

"Come off it, Ace," I interrupted. "I havent got anything against Barbara. The shoe is on the other foot. Tell her I'm all right, will you? Don't waste time trying to convince me; I'm just trying to get along."

It was clear, not only from the slips which evaded Ace's guard, but from less restrained remarks by other fellows, that Barbara's tortured jealousy was a fixture of her character. She had created feuds, slandered and reviled fellows who had been guilty of nothing except trying to interest her father in some project in which she herself was not concerned. I learned much more also, much Ace had no desire to convey. But he was a poor hand at concealing anything, and it was clear he was helplessly subject to her, but without the usual kindly anesthetic of illusion. I guessed he had enjoyed her favors, but she evidently didnt bother to hide the fact that the privilege was not exclusive; perhaps indeed she insisted on his knowing. I gathered she was a fiercely moral polyandrist, demanding absolute fidelity without offering the slightest hope of reciprocal singlemindedness.

12. MORE OF HAGGERSHAVEN

$\mathcal{A}$MONG THE FELLOWS was an Oliver Midbin, a student of what he chose to call the new and revolutionary science of Emotional Pathology. Tall and thin, with an incongruous little potbelly like an enlarged and far-slipped adamsapple, he pounced on me as a readymade and captive audience for his theories.

"Now this case of pseudo-aphonia—"

"He means the dumb girl," explained Ace, aside.

"Nonsense. Dumbness is not even the statement of a symptom, but a very imperfect description. Pseudo-aphonia. Purely of an emotional nature. Of course if you take her to some medical quack he'll convince himself and you and certainly her that there's an impairment, or degeneration, or atrophy of the vocal cords—"

"I'm not the girl's guardian, Mr Midbin—"

"Doctor. Philosophiae, Göttingen. Trivial matter."

"Excuse me, Dr Midbin. Anyway, I'm not her guardian so I'm not taking her anywhere. But, just as a theoretical question, suppose examination did reveal physical damage?"

He appeared delighted, and rubbed his hands together. "Oh, it would. I assure you it would. These fellows always find what theyre looking for. If your disposition is sour theyll find warts on your duodenum. In a postmortem. In a postmortem. Whereas Emotional Pathology deals with the sour disposition and lets the warts, if any, take care of themselves. Matter is a function of the mind. People are dumb or blind or deaf for a purpose. Now what purpose can the girl have for muteness?"

"No conversation?" I suggested. I didnt doubt Midbin was an authority, but his manner made flippancy almost irresistible.

"I shall find out," he said firmly. "This is bound to be a simpler maladjustment than Barbara's—"

"Aw, come on," protested Ace.

"Nonsense, Dorn; obscurantic nonsense. Reticence is a necessary ingredient of those medical ethics by which the quacks conceal incompetence. Mumbo jumbo to keep the layman from asking annoying questions. Priestly, not scientific approach. Art and mystery of phlebotomy. Don't hold back knowledge; publish it to the world."

"I think Barbara wouldnt want her private thoughts published to the world. You have to draw the line somewhere."

Midbin put his head on one side and looked at Ace as though he were difficult to see. "Now that's interesting, Dorn," he said; "I wonder what turns a seeker after knowledge into a censor."

"Are you going to start exploring my emotional pathology now?"

"Not interesting enough; not nearly interesting enough. Diagnosis while you wait; treatment in a few easy instalments. Barbara now—there's a really beautiful case. Beautiful case; years of treatment and little sign of improvement. Of course she wouldnt want her thoughts known. Why? Because she's happy with her hatred for her dead mother. Shocking to Mrs Grundy; doubly ditto to Mister. Exaggerated possessiveness toward her father makes her miserable. Thoughts known, misery ventilated: shame, condemnation, fie, fie. Her fantasy—"

"Midbin!"

"Her fantasy of going back to childhood (fascinating; adult employs infantile time-sequence, infantile magic, infantile hatreds) in order to injure her mother is a sick notion she cherishes the way a dog licks a wound. But without analogous therapy. Ventilate it. Ventilate it. Now this girl's case is bound to be simpler. Younger if nothing else. And nice, overt symptoms. Bring her around tomorrow and we'll begin."

"Me?" I asked.

"Who else? Youre the only one she doesnt seem to distrust."

It was annoying to have the girl's puppylike devotion observed and commented on. I realized she saw me as the only connection, however tenuous, with a normal past; I had assumed she would turn naturally after a few days to the women who took such open pleasure in fussing over her affliction. However she merely suffered their attentions; no matter how I tried to avoid her she sought me out, running to me with muted cries which should have been touching but were only painful.

Mr Haggerwells' telegram to the sheriff's office at York had brought the reply that a deputy sheriff would visit the haven "when time permitted." He had also telegraphed the Spanish legation who answered they knew no other Escobars than Don Jaime and his wife. The girl might be a servant or a stranger; it was no concern of His Most Catholic Majesty.

The school uniform made it unlikely she was a servant but beyond this, little was deducible. She did not respond to questions in either Spanish or English, and it was impossible to tell if she understood their meaning, for her blank expression remained unchanged. When offered pencil and paper she handled them curiously, then let them slide to the floor.

I wondered briefly if perhaps her intelligence was slightly subnormal, but this was met by a firm, even belligerent denial from Midbin, whose conclusion was confirmed, at least in my opinion, by her apparently excellent coordination, her personal neatness and fastidiousness which were far more delicate than any I'd been accustomed to.

Midbin's method of treatment smacked of the mystical. His subjects were supposed to relax on a couch and say whatever came into their minds. At least this was the clearest part of the explanation he gave when I rebelliously escorted the girl to his "office," a large, bare room decorated only by some old European calendars by the popular academician, Picasso. The couch was a cot which Midbin himself used more conventionally at night.

"All right," I said; "just how are you going to manage?"

"Convince her everything's all right and I'm not going to hurt her."

"Sure," I agreed. "Sure. Only: how?"

He gave me one of his head-on-shoulder looks and turned to the girl who waited apathetically, with downcast eyes. "You lie down," he suggested.

"Me? I'm not dumb."

"Pretend you are. Lie down, close your eyes, say the first thing on your tongue. Without stopping to think about it."

"How can I say anything if I'm pretending to be dumb?" Grudgingly I complied, fancying a faint look of curiosity passing over the too-placid face. " 'No man bathes twice in the same stream,' " I muttered.

He made me repeat the performance several times, then by pantomime urged her to imitate me. It was doubtful if she understood; in the end we nudged her gently into the required position. There was no question of relaxation; she lay there warily, tense and stiff even with her eyes closed.

The whole business was so manifestly useless and absurd, to say nothing of being undignified, that I was tempted to walk out on it. Only ignoble calculation on Midbin's voting for my acceptance in the haven kept me there.

Looking at the form stretched out so rigidly, I could not but admit again that the girl was beautiful. But the admission was dispassionate; the beauty was abstract and neutral, the lovely young lines evoked no lust. I felt only vexation because her plight kept me from the wonders of Haggershaven.

"What good can this possibly do?" I burst out after ten fruitless minutes. "Youre trying to find out why she can't talk and she can't talk to tell you why she can't talk."

"Science explores all methods of approach," Midbin answered loftily; "I'm searching for a technique which will reach her. Bring her back tomorrow."

I swallowed my annoyance and started out. The girl jumped up and pressed close to my side. Outdoors the air was crisp; I felt her suppress a slight shiver. "Now I suppose I'll have to take you where it's warm or find a wrap for you," I scolded irritably. "I don't know why I have to be your nursemaid."

She whimpered very softly and I was remorseful. None of this was her fault; my callousness was inexcusable. But if she could only attach herself to some other protector and leave me alone . . .

As one about to be banished I tried to cram everything into short days. I realized that these autumn weeks, spent in casual conversation or joining the familiar preparations for rural winter, were a period of thorough and critical probation. There was little I could do to sway the decision beyond the exhibition of an honest willingness to turn to whatever work needed doing, and to repeat, whenever the opportunity offered, that Haggershaven was literally a revelation to me, an island of civilization in the midst of a chaotic and savage sea. My dream was to make a landfall there.

Certainly my meager background and scraps of reading would not persuade the men and women of the haven; I could only hope they might divine some promise in me. Against this hope I put Barbara's enmity, a hostility now exacerbated by rage at Oliver Midbin for daring to devote to another, particularly another woman, the attention which had been her due, and the very technique used for her. I knew her persistence and I could not doubt she would move enough of the fellows to insure my rejection.

The gang which had been operating in the vicinity, presumably the same one I had encountered, moved on. At least no further crimes were attributed to it. Once they were gone, Deputy Sheriff Beasley finally found time to visit Haggershaven in response to the telegram. He had evidently been there before without attaining much respect on either side. I got the distinct impression he would have preferred a more formal examination than the one which took place in Mr Haggerwells' study, with fellows drifting in and out, interrupting the proceedings with comments of their own.

I think he doubted the girl's dumbness. He barked his questions so loudly and brusquely they would have terrified a far more securely poised individual. She promptly went into dry hysterics, whereupon he turned his attention to me.

I was apprehensive lest his questions explore my life with Tyss and my connection with the Grand Army, but apparently mere presence at Haggershaven indicated an innocence not unrelated to idiocy, at least so far as the more popular crimes were concerned. My passage of the York road and all the events leading up to it were outside his interest; he wanted only a succinct story of the holdup, reminding me of the late Colonel Tolliburr in his assumption that the lay eye ought normally to be photographic of the minutest detail.

He was clearly dissatisfied with my account and left grumbling that it would be more to the point if bookworms learned to identify a man properly, instead of logarithms or trigonometry. I didn't see exactly how this applied to me, since I was laudably ignorant of both subjects.

If Officer Beasley was disappointed, Midbin was enchanted. Of course he had heard my narrative before, but this was the first time he'd savored its possible impact on the girl.

"You see, her pseudo-aphonia is neither congenital nor of long standing. All logic leads to the conclusion that it's the result of her terror during the experience. She must have wanted to scream, it must have been almost impossible for her not to scream, but for her very life she dared not. The instinctive, automatic reaction was the one she could not allow herself. She had to remain mute while she watched the murders."

For the first time it seemed possible there was more to Midbin than his garrulity.

"She crushed back that natural, overwhelming impulse," he went on. "She had to; her life depended on it. It was an enormous effort and the effect on her was in proportion; she achieved her object too well; when it was safe for her to speak again she couldnt."

It all sounded so plausible it was some time before I thought to ask him why she didnt appear to understand what we said, or why she didnt write anything when she was handed pencil and paper.

"Communication," he answered. "She had to cut off communication, and once cut off it's not easy to restore. At least that's one aspect. Another is more tricky. The holdup happened more than a month ago, but do you suppose the affected mind reckons so precisely? Is a precise reckoning possible? Duration may, for all we know, be an entirely subjective thing. Yesterday for you may be today for me. We recognize this to some extent when we speak of hours passing slowly or quickly. The girl may still be undergoing the agony of repressing her screams; the holdup, the murders, are not in the past for her, but the present. They are taking place in a long drawn out instant of time which may never end during her life. And if this is so, is it any wonder she is unable to relax, to let down her guard long enough to realize that the present is present and the crisis is past?"

He pressed his middle thoughtfully. "Now, if it is possible to recreate in her mind by stimulus from without rather than by evocation from within the conditions leading up to and through the climacteric, she would have a chance to vent the emotions she was forced to swallow. She might, I don't say she would, she might speak again."

I understood such a process would necessarily be lengthy, but as time passed I saw no indication he was reaching her at all, much less that he was getting any results. One of the Spanish-speaking fellows, a botanist who came and went from the haven at erratic intervals, translated my account of our meeting and read parts of it to the recumbent girl, following Midbin's excited stage directions and interpolations. Nothing happened.

Outside the futile duty of coaxing the girl to participate in Midbin's sessions I had no obligations except those I took upon myself or could persuade others to delegate to me. Hiro Agati declared me hopelessly incompetent to help him in the kiln he had set up to make "hard glass," a thick substance he hoped might take the place of cast iron in such things as woodstoves, or clay tile in flues. He conceded I was not entirely useless in the small garden surrounding their cottage where he, Mrs Agati—an architect, much younger than her husband and extremely diminutive—and their three children spent their spare time transplanting, rearranging, or preparing for the following season.

Dr Agati was not only the first American Japanese I had ever met; his was the first family I had known who broke the unwritten rule of having only one child. Both he and Kimi Agati seemed unaware of the stern injunctions by Whigs and Populists alike that disaster would follow if the population of the country increased too fast. Fumio and Eiko didnt care, while Yoshio, at two, was just not interested.

The Agatis represented for me one more pang at the thought of banishment from the haven. Since I knew neither chemistry nor architecture, our conversation had limits, but this was no drawback to the pleasure I took in their company. Often, after I was assured I was welcome there, I sat reading or simply silent while Hiro worked, the children ran in and out, and Kimi, who was conservative and didnt care for chairs, sat comfortably on the floor and sketched or calculated stresses.

Gradually I progressed from the stage where I wanted decision on my application postponed as long as possible to one where I was impatient to have it over and done with. "Why?" asked Hiro. "Suspense is the condition we live in all our lives."

"Well, but there are degrees. You know about what you will be doing next year."

"Do I? What guarantees have I? The future is happily veiled. When I was your age I despaired because no one would accept the indentures of a Japanese. (We are still called Japanese even though our ancestors migrated at the time of the abortive attempt to overthrow the Shogunate and restore the Mikado in 1868.) Suspense instead of certainty would have been a pleasure."

"Anyway," said Kimi practically, "it may be months before the next meeting."

"What do you mean? Isnt there a set time for such business?" Sure there must be, I had never dared ask the exact date.

Hiro shook his head. "Why should there be? The next time the fellows pass on an appropriation or a project, we'll decide whether there's room for an historian."

"But . . . as Kimi says, it might not be for months."

"Or it might be tomorrow," replied Hiro.

"Don't worry, Hodge," said Fumio, "Papa will vote for you, and Mother too."

Hiro grunted.

When it did come it was anticlimactic. Hiro, Midbin, and several others with whom I'd scarcely exchanged a word recommended me, and Barbara simply ignored my existence. I was a full fellow of Haggershaven, with all the duties and privileges appertaining. I was also securely at home for the first time since I left Wappinger Falls more than six years before. I knew that in all its history few had ever cut themselves off from the haven, still fewer had ever been asked to resign.

At a modest celebration in the big kitchen that night, the haven revealed more of the talents it harbored. Hiro produced a gallon of liquor he had distilled from sawdust and called cellusaki. Mr Haggerwells pronounced it fit for a cultivated palate, following with an impromptu discourse on drinking through the ages. Midbin sampled enough of it to imitate Mr. Haggerwells' lecture and then, as an inspired afterthought, to demonstrate how Mr Haggerwells might mimic Midbin's parody. Ace and three others sang ballads; even the dumb girl, persuaded to sip a little of the cellusaki under the disapproving eyes of her self-appointed guardians, seemed to become faintly animated. If anyone noted the absence of Barbara Haggerwells, no one commented on it.

Fall became winter. Surplus timber was hauled in from the woodlots and the lignin extracted by compressed air, a method perfected by one of the fellows. Lignin was the fuel used in our hot water furnaces and provided the gas for the reflecting jets which magnified a tiny flame into strong illumination. All of us took part in this work, but just as I had not been able to help Hiro to his satisfaction in the laboratory, so here too my ineptness with things mechanical soon caused me to be set to more congenial tasks in the stables.

I did not repine at this, for though I was delighted with the society of the others, I found it pleasurable to be alone, to sort out my thoughts, to slow down to the rhythm of the heavy percherons or enjoy the antics of the two young foals. The world and time were somewhere shut outside; I felt contentment so strong as to be beyond satisfaction or any active emotion.

I was currying a dappled mare one afternoon and reflecting how the steam-plow used on the great wheat ranches of British America deprived the farmers not merely of fertilizer but also of companionship, when Barbara, her breath still cloudy from the cold outside, came in and stood behind me. I made an artificial cowlick on the mare's flank, then brushed it glossy smooth again.

"Hello," she said.

"Uh . . . hello, Miss Haggerwells."

"Must you, Hodge?"

I roughed up the mare's flank once more. "Must I what? I'm afraid I don't understand."

She came close, as close as she had in the bookstore, and I felt my breath quicken. "I think you do. Why do you avoid me? And call me 'Miss Haggerwells' in that prim tone? Do I look so old and ugly and forbidding?"

This, I thought, is going to hurt Ace. Poor Ace, befuddled by a Jezebel; why can't he attach himself to a nice quiet girl who won't tear him in pieces every time she follows her inclinations?

I smoothed the mare's side for the last time and put down the currycomb.

"I think you are the most exciting woman Ive ever met, Barbara," I said.

13. TIME

"*H*ODGE."

"Barbara?"

"Is it really true youve never written your mother since you left home?"

"Why should I write her? What could I say? Perhaps if my first plans had come to something, I might have. But to tell her I worked for six years for nothing would only confirm her opinion of my lack of gumption."

"I wonder if your ambitions in the end don't amount to a wish to prove her wrong."

"Now you sound like Midbin," I said, but I wasnt annoyed. I much preferred her present questions to those I'd heard from her in the past weeks: Do you love me? Are you sure? Really love, I mean; more than any other woman? Why?

"Oliver has had accidental flashes of insight."

"Arent you substituting your own for what you think might be my motives?"

"My mother hated me," she stated flatly.

"Well, it isnt a world where love is abundant; substitutes are cheap and available. But hate—that's a strong word. How do you know?"

"I know. What does it matter how? I'm not unfeeling, like you."

"Me? Now what have I done?"

"You don't care about anyone. Not me or anyone else. You don't want me; just any woman would do."

I considered this. "I don't think so, Barbara—"

"See! You don't think so. Youre not sure, and anyway you wouldnt hurt my feelings needlessly. Why don't you be honest and tell the truth. You'd just as soon it was that streetwalker in New York. Maybe you'd rather. You miss her, don't you?"

"Barbara, Ive told you a dozen times I never—"

"And Ive told you a dozen times youre a liar! I don't care. I really don't care."

"All right."

"How can you be so phlegmatic? So unfeeling? Nothing means anything to you. Youre a real, stolid peasant. And you smell like one too, always reeking of the stable."

"I'm sorry," I said mildly; "I'll try to bathe more often."

Her taunts and jealous fits, her insistent demands did not ruffle me. I was too pleased with the wonders of life to be disturbed. All I'd dreamed Haggershaven could mean when I was sure I would never be part of it was fulfilled and more than fulfilled. Haggershaven and Barbara; Eden and Lilith.

At first it seemed the bookstore years were wasted, but I soon realized the value of that catholic and serendipitous reading as a preparation for this time. I was momentarily disappointed that there was no one at the haven to whom I could turn for that personal, face-to-face, student-teacher relationship on which I'd set so great a store, but if there was no historical scholar among the fellows to tutor me, I was surrounded by those who had learned the discipline of study. There was none to discuss the details of the industrial revolution or the failure of the Ultramontane Movement in Catholicism and the policies of Popes Adrian VII, VIII and IX, but all could show me scheme and method. I began to understand what thorough exploration of a subject meant as opposed to sciolism, and I threw myself into my chosen work with furious zest.

I also began to understand the central mystery of historical theory. When and what and how and where, but the when is the least. Not chronology but relationship is ultimately what the historian deals in. The element of time, so vital at first glance, assumes a constantly more subordinate character. That the past is past becomes ever less important. Except for perspective it might as well be the present or the future or, if one can conceive it, a parallel time. I was not investigating a petrification but a fluid. Were it possible to know fully the what and how and where one might learn the why, and assuredly if one grasped the why he could place the when at will.

During that winter I read philosophy, psychology, archaeology, anthropology. My energy and appetite were prodigious, as they needed to be. I saw the field of knowledge, not knowledge in the abstract, but things I wanted to know, things I had to know, expanding in front of me with dizzying speed while I crawled and crept and stumbled over ground I should have covered years before.

Yet if I had studied more conventionally I would never have had the Haven or Barbara. Novelists speak lightly of gusts of passion, but it was nothing less than irresistible force which drove me to her, day after day. Looking back on what I had felt for Tirzah Vame with the condescension twenty-four has toward twenty, I saw my younger self only as callow, boyish and slightly obtuse. I was embarrassed by the torments I had suffered.

With Barbara I lived only in the present, shutting out past and future. This was only partly due to the intensity, the fierceness of our desire; much came from Barbara's own troubled spirit. She herself was so avid, so demanding, that yesterday and tomorrow were irrelevant to the insistent moment. The only thing saving me from enslavement like poor Ace was the belief, correct or incorrect I am to this day not certain, that to yield the last vestige of detachment and objectivity would make me helpless, not just before her, but to accomplish my ever more urgent ambitions.

Still I know much of my reserve was unnecessary, a product of fear, not prudence. I denied much I could have given freely and without harm; my guard protected what was essentially empty. My fancied advantage over Ace, based on my having always had an easy, perhaps too easy way with women, was no advantage at all. I foolishly thought myself master of the situation because her infidelities, if such a word can be used where faithfulness is explicitly ruled out, did not bother me. I believed I had grown immensely wise since the time when the prospect of Tirzah's rejection had made me miserable. I was wrong; my sophistication was a lack, not an achievement.

Do I need to say that Barbara was no wanton, moved by light and fickle voluptuousness? The puritanism of our time, expressing itself in condemnations and denials, molded her as it molded our civilization. She was driven by urges deeper and darker than sensuality; her mad jealousies were provoked by an unappeasable need for constant reassurance. She had to be dominant, she had to be courted by more than one man; she had to be told constantly what she could never truly believe: that she was uniquely desired.

I wondered that she did not burn herself out, not only with conflicting passions, but with her fury of work. Sleep was a weakness she despised, yet she craved far more of it than she allowed herself; she rationed her hours of unconsciousness and drove herself relentlessly. Ace's panegyrics on her importance as a physicist I discounted, but older and more objective colleagues spoke of her mathematical concepts, not merely with respect, but with awe.

She did not discuss her work with me; our intimacy stopped short of such exchanges. I got the impression she was seeking the principles of heavier-than-air flight, a chimera which had long intrigued inventors. It seemed a pointless pursuit, for it was manifest such levitation could no more replace our safe, comfortable guided balloons than minibiles could replace the horse.

Spring made all of us single-minded farmers until the fields were plowed and sown. No one grudged these days, for the Haven's economic life was based first of all on its land, and we were happy in the work itself. Not until the most feverish competition with time began to slacken could we return to our regular activities.

I say "all of us," but I must except the dumb girl. She greeted the spring with the nearest approach to cheerfulness she had displayed; there was a distinct lifting of her apathy. Unexpectedly she revealed a talent which had survived the shock to her personality or had been resurrected

like the pussywillows and crocuses by the warm sun. She
was a craftsman with needle and thread. Timidly at first,
but gradually growing bolder, she contrived dresses of
gayer and gayer colors in place of the drab school uniform;
always, on the completion of a new creation, running to
me as though to solicit my approval.

This innocent if embarrassing custom could hardly escape Barbara's notice, but her anger was directed at me,
not the girl. My "devotion" was not only absurd, she told
me, it was also conspicuous and degrading. My taste was
inexplicable, running as it did to immature, deranged
cripples.

Naturally when the girl took up the habit of coming to
the edge of the field where I was plowing, waiting gravely
motionless for me to drive the furrow toward her, I anticipated still further punishment from Barbara's tongue. The
girl was not to be swayed from her practice; at least I did
not have the heart to speak roughly to her, and so she daily
continued to stand through the long hours watching me
plow, bringing me a lunch at noon and docilely sharing a
small portion of it.

The planting done, Midbin began the use of a new technique, showing her drawings of successive stages of the
holdup, again nagging and pumping me for details to
sharpen their accuracy. Her reactions pleased him immensely, for she responded to the first ones with nods and
the throaty sounds we recognized as understanding or
agreement. The scenes of the assault itself, of the shooting
of the coachman, the flight of the footman, and her own
concealment in the cornfield evoked whimpers, while the
brutal depiction of the Escobars' murder made her cower
and cover her eyes.

I suppose I am not particularly tactful; still I had been
careful not to mention any of this to Barbara. Midbin, however, after a very gratifying reaction to one of the drawings,
said casually, "Barbara hasnt been here for a long time. I
wish she would come back."

When I repeated this she stormed at me. "How dare
you discuss me with that ridiculous fool?"

"Youve got it all wrong. There wasnt any discussion. Midbin only said—"

"I know what Oliver said. I know his whole silly vocabulary."

"He only wants to help you."

"Help me? Help *me?* What's wrong with me?"

"Nothing, Barbara. Nothing."

"Am I dumb or blind or stupid?"

"Please, Barbara."

"Just unattractive. I know. Ive seen you with that creature. How you must hate me to flaunt her before everyone!"

"You know I only go with her to Midbin's because he insists."

"What about your little lovers' meetings in the woodlot when you were supposed to be plowing? Do you think I didnt know about them?"

"Barbara, I assure you they were perfectly harmless. She—"

"Youre a liar. More than that, youre a sneak and a hypocrite. Yes, and a mean, crawling sycophant as well. I know you must detest me, but it suits you to suffer me because of the haven. I'm not blind; youve used me, deliberately and calculatedly for your own selfish ends."

Midbin could explain and excuse her outbursts by his "emotional pathology," Ace accepted and suffered them as inescapable, so did her father, but I saw no necessity of being always subject to her tantrums. I told her so, adding, not too heatedly I think, "Maybe we shouldnt see each other alone after this."

She stood perfectly immobile and silent, as if I were still speaking. "All right," she said at last. "All right; yes . . . yes. Don't."

Her apparent calm deceived me completely; I smiled with relief.

"That's right, laugh. Why shouldnt you? You have no feelings, no more than you have an intelligence. You are an oaf, a clod, a real bumpkin. Standing there with a silly grin on your face. Oh I hate you! How I hate you!"

She wept, she shrilled, she rushed at me and then turned

away, crying she hadnt meant it, not a word of it. She cajoled, begging forgiveness for all she'd said, tearfully promising to control herself after this, moaning that she needed me, and finally, when I didnt repulse her, exclaiming it was her love for me which tormented her so and drove her to such scenes. It was a wretched, degrading moment, and not the least of its wretchedness and degradation was that I recognized the erotic value of her abjection. Detachedly I might pity, fear or be repelled; at the same time I had to admit her sudden humility was exciting.

Perhaps this storm changed our relationship for the better, or at least eased the constraint between us. At any rate it was after this she began speaking to me of her work, putting us on a friendlier, less furious plane. I learned now how completely garbled was my notion of what she was doing.

"Heavier-than-air flying-machines!" she cried. "How utterly absurd!"

"All right. I didnt know."

"My work is theoretical. I'm not a vulgar mechanic."

"All right, all right."

"I'm going to show that time and space are aspects of the same entity."

"All right," I said, thinking of something else.

"What is time?"

"Uh? . . . Dear Barbara, since I don't know anything I can slide gracefully out of that one. I couldnt even begin to define time."

"Oh, you could probably define it all right—in terms of itself. I'm not dealing with definitions but concepts."

"All right, conceive."

"Hodge, like all stuffy people your levity is ponderous."

"Excuse me. Go ahead."

"Time is an aspect."

"So you mentioned. I once knew a man who said it was an illusion. And another who said it was a serpent with its tail in its mouth."

"Mysticism." The contempt with which she spoke the word brought a sudden image of Roger Tyss saying "metaphysics" with much the same inflection. "Time, matter, space and energy are all aspects of the cosmic entity. Interchangeable aspects. Theoretically it should be possible to translate matter into terms of energy and space into terms of time; matter-energy into space-time."

"It sounds so simple I'm ashamed of myself."

"To put it so crudely the explanation is misleading: suppose matter is resolved into its component . . ."

"Atoms?" I suggested, since she seemed at loss for a word.

"No, atoms are already too individualized, too separate. Something more fundamental than atoms. We have no word because we can't quite grasp the concept yet. Essence, perhaps, or the theological 'spirit.' If matter . . ."

"A man?"

"Man, turnip or chemical compound," she answered impatiently; "is resolved into its essence it can presumably be reassembled, another wrong word, at another point of the time-space fabric."

"You mean . . . like yesterday?"

"No—and yes. What is 'yesterday'? A thing? An aspect? An idea? Or a relationship? Oh, words are useless things; even with mathematical symbols you can hardly . . . But someday I'll establish it. Or lay the groundwork for my successors. Or the successors of my successors."

I nodded. Midbin was at least half right; Barbara was emotionally sick. For what was this "theory" of hers but the rationalization of a daydream, the daydream of discovering a process for reaching back through time to injure her dead mother and so steal all of her father's affections?

14. MIDBIN'S EXPERIMENT

*A*T THE NEXT meeting of the fellows Midbin asked an appropriation for experimental work and the help of haven members in the project. Since the extent of both requests was modest, their granting would ordinarily have been a formality. But Barbara asked politely if Dr Midbin wouldnt like to elaborate a little on the purposes of his experiment.

I knew her manner was a danger signal. Nevertheless Midbin merely answered goodhumoredly that he proposed to test a theory of whether an emotionally induced physical handicap could be cured by recreating in the subject's mind the shock which had caused—to use a loose, inaccurate term—the impediment.

"I thought so. He wants to waste the haven's money and time on a little tart he's having an affair with while important work is held up for lack of funds."

One of the women called out, "Oh, Barbara, no," and there were exclamations of disapproval. I saw Kimi Agati look steadfastly down in embarrassment. Mr Haggerwells, after trying unsuccessfully to hold Barbara's eye, said, "I must apologize for my daughter—"

"It's all right," interrupted Midbin. "I understand Barbara's notions. I'm sure no one here really thinks there is anything improper between the girl and me. Outside of this, Barbara's original question seems quite in order. Quite in order. Briefly, as most of you know, Ive been trying to restore speech to a subject who lost it—again I use an inaccurate term for convenience—during an afflicting experience. Preliminary explorations indicate good probability of satisfactory response to my proposed method, which is simply to employ a kinematic camera like those making entertainment photinugraphs—"

"He wants to turn the haven into a tinugraph mill with the fellows as mummers!"

"Only this once, Barbara, only this once. Not regularly; not as routine."

At this point her father insisted the request be voted on without any more discussion. I was tempted to vote with Barbara, the only dissident, for I foresaw Midbin's tinugraph would undoubtedly rely heavily on cooperation from me, but I didnt have the courage. Instead I merely abstained, like Midbin himself and Ace.

The first effect of Midbin's program was to free me from obligation, for he decided there was no point continuing the sessions with the dumb girl as before. All his time was taken up anyway with photography—no one at the haven had specialized in it—kinematic theory, the art of pantomime, and the relative merit of different makes of cameras, all manufactured abroad.

The girl, who had never lost her tenseness and apprehension during the interviews, nevertheless clung to the habit of being escorted to Midbin's workroom. Since it was impossible to convey to her that the sessions were temporarily suspended, she appeared regularly, always in a dress with which she had taken manifest pains, and there was little I could do but walk her to Midbin's and back. I was acutely conscious of the ridiculousness of these parades and expectant of retribution from Barbara afterward, so I was to some extent relieved when Midbin finally made his decision and procured camera and film.

Now I had to set the exact scene where the holdup had taken place, not an easy thing to do, for one rise looks much like another at twilight and all look differently in daylight. Then I had to approximate the original conditions as nearly as possible. Here Midbin was partially foiled by the limitations of his medium, being forced to use the camera in full sunlight instead of at dusk.

I dressed and instructed the actors in their parts, rehears-

ing and directing them throughout. The only immunity I
got was Midbin's concession that I neednt play the role of
myself, since in my early part of spectator I would be hidden anyway, and the succor was omitted as irrelevant to
the therapeutic purpose. Midbin himself did nothing but
tend the camera.

Any tinugraph mill would have snorted at our final product and certainly no tinugraph lyceum would have conde-
scended to show it. After some hesitation Midbin had decided not to make a phonoto, feeling the use of sound
would add no value and considerable expense, so the film
didnt even have this feature to recommend it. Fortunately
for whatever involuntary professional pride was involved,
no one was present at the first showing but the girl and me,
Ace to work the magic-lantern, and Midbin.

In the darkened room the pictures on the screen gave—
after the first minutes—such an astonishing illusion that
when one of the horsemen rode toward the camera we all
reflexively shrank back. Despite its amateurishness the tinugraph seemed an artistic success to us, but it was no triumph in justifying its existence. The girl reacted no differently than she had toward the drawings; if anything her
response was less satisfactory. The inarticulate noises ran
the same scale from dismay to terror; nothing new was
added. Nevertheless Midbin, his adamsapple working joy-
ously up and down, slapped Ace and me on the back, pre-
dicting he'd have her talking like a politician before the
year was out.

I suppose the process was imperceptible; certainly there
was no discernible difference between one showing and the
next. The boring routine continued day after day and so
absolute was Midbin's confidence that we were not too
astonished after some weeks when, at the moment "Don
Jaime" folded in simulated death, she fainted and remained
unconscious for some time.

After this we expected—at least Ace and I did, Midbin
only rubbed his palms together—that the constraint on her
tongue would be suddenly and entirely lifted. It wasnt, but
a few showings later, at the same crucial point, she

screamed. It was a genuine scream, clear and piercing, bearing small resemblance to the strangling noises we were accustomed to. Midbin had been vindicated; no mute could have voiced that full, shrill cry.

Pursuing another of his theories, he soon gave up the idea of helping her express the words in her mind in Spanish. Instead he concentrated on teaching her English. His method was primitive, consisting of pointing solemnly to objects and repeating their names in an artificial monotone.

"She'll have an odd way of speaking," remarked Ace; "all nouns, singular nouns at that, said with a mouthful of pebbles. I can just imagine the happy day: 'Man chair wall girl floor;' and you bubbling back, 'Carpet ceiling earth grass.' "

"I'll supply the verbs as needed," said Midbin; "first things first."

She must have been paying at least as much attention to our conversation as to his instruction for, unexpectedly, one day she pointed to me and said quite clearly, "Hodge . . . Hodge . . ."

I was discomposed, but not with the same vexation I had felt at her habit of seeking me out and following me around. There was a faint, bashful pleasure, and a feeling of gratitude for such steadfastness.

She must have had some grounding in English, for while she utilized the nouns Midbin had supplied, she soon added, tentatively and questioningly, a verb or adjective here and there. "I . . . walk . . .?" Ace's fear of her acquiring Midbin's dead inflection was groundless; her voice was low and charmingly modulated; we were enchanted listening to her elementary groping among words.

Conversation or questioning was as yet impossible. Midbin's, "What is your name?" brought forth no response save a puzzled look and a momentary sinking back into dullness. But several weeks later she touched her breast and said shyly, "Catalina."

Her memory then, was not impaired, at least not totally. There was no way of telling yet what she remembered and what self-protection had forced her to forget, for direct questions seldom brought satisfactory answers at this stage.

Facts concerning herself she gave out sporadically and without relation to our curiosity.

Her name was Catalina García; she was the much younger sister of Doña Maria Escobar, with whom she lived. So far as she knew she had no other relatives. She did not want to go back to school; they had taught her to sew, they had been kind, but she had not been happy there. Please—we would not send her away from Haggershaven, would we?

Midbin acted now like a fond parent who was both proud of his child's accomplishments and fearful lest she be not quite ready to leave his solicitous care. He was far from satisfied at restoring her speech; he probed and searched, seeking to know what she had thought and felt during the long months of muteness.

"I do not know, truly I do not know," she protested toward the end of one of these examinations. "I would say, yes; sometimes I knew you were talking to me, or Hodge." Here she looked at me steadily for an instant, to make me feel both remorseful and proud. "But it was like someone talking a long way off, so I never quite understood, nor was even sure it was I who was being spoken to. Often—at least it seemed often, perhaps it was not—often, I tried to speak, to beg you to tell me if you were real people talking to me, or just part of a dream. That was very bad, because when no words came I was more afraid than ever, and when I was afraid the dream became darker and darker."

Afterward, looking cool and fresh and strangely assured, she came upon me while I was cultivating young corn. A few weeks earlier I would have known she had sought me out; now it might be an accident.

"But I knew more surely when it was you who spoke, Hodge," she said abruptly. "In my dream you were the most real." Then she walked tranquilly away.

Barbara, who had studiedly said nothing further about what Midbin was doing, commented one day, apparently without rancor, "So Oliver appears to have proved a theory. How nice for you."

"What do you mean?" I inquired guardedly; "How is it nice for me?"

"Why, you won't have to chaperone the silly girl all over any more. She can ask her way around now."

"Oh yes; that's right," I mumbled.

"And we won't have to quarrel over her any more," she concluded.

"Sure," I said. "That's right."

Mr Haggerwells again communicated with the Spanish diplomats, recalling his original telegram and mentioning the aloof reply. He was answered in person by an official who acted as though he himself had composed the disclaiming response. Perhaps he had, for he made it quite clear that only devotion to duty made it possible to deal at all with such savages as inhabited the United States.

He confirmed the existence of one Catalina García and consulted a photograph, carefully shielded in his hand, comparing it with the features of our Catalina, at last satisfying himself they were the same. This formality finished, he spoke rapidly to Catalina in Spanish. She shook her head and looked confused. "Tell him I can hardly understand, Hodge; ask him to speak in English, please."

The diplomat looked furious. Midbin explained hastily that the shock which had caused her muteness had not entirely worn off. Unquestionably she would recover her full memory in time, but for the present there were still areas of forgetfulness. Her native language was part of the past, he went on, happy with a new audience, and the past was something to be pushed away since it contained the terrible moment. English on the other hand—"

"I understand," said the diplomat stiffly, resolutely addressing none of us. "It is clear. Very well then. The Señorita García is heir—heiress to an estate. Not a very big one, I regret to say. A moderate estate."

"You mean land and houses?" I asked curiously.

"A moderate estate," he repeated, looking attentively at his gloved hand. "Some shares of stock, some bonds, some cash. The details will be available to the señorita."

"It doesnt matter," said Catalina timidly.

Having put us all, and particularly me, in our place as rude and nosey barbarians, he went on more pleasantly, "According to the records of the embassy, the señorita is not yet eighteen. As an orphan living in foreign lands she is a ward of the Spanish Crown. The señorita will return with me to Philadelphia where she will be suitably accommodated until repatriation can be arranged. I feel certain that in the proper surroundings, hearing her natural tongue, she will soon regain its use. The—ah—institution may submit a bill for board and lodging during her stay."

"Does he mean—take me away from here? For always?" Catalina, who had seemed so mature a moment before, suddenly acted like a frightened child.

"He only wants to make you comfortable and take you among your own people," said Mr Haggerwells. "Perhaps it is a bit sudden . . ."

"I can't. Do not let him take me away. Hodge, Hodge—do not let him take me away."

"Señorita, you do not understand—"

"No, no. I won't. Hodge, Mr Haggerwells, do not let him!"

"But my dear—"

It was Midbin who cut Mr Haggerwells off. "I cannot guarantee against a relapse, even a reversion to the pseudo-aphonia if this emotional tension is maintained: I must insist that Catalina is not to continue the conversation now."

"No one's going to take you away by force," I assured her, finally finding my courage once Midbin had asserted himself.

The official shrugged, managing to intimate in the gesture his opinion that the haven was of a very shady character indeed and had quite possibly engineered the holdup itself.

"If the señorita genuinely wishes to remain for the present—" a lifted eyebrow loaded the "genuinely" with meaning "—I have no authority at the moment to inquire into influences that have persuaded her. No, none at all. Nor can I remove her by—ah—I will not insist. No. Not at all."

"That is very understanding of you, sir," said Mr Haggerwells. "I'm sure everything will be all right eventually."

The diplomat bowed stiffly. "Of course the—ah—institution understands it can hope for no further compensation—"

"None has been given or asked for. None will be," said Mr Haggerwells in what was, for him, a sharp tone.

The gentleman from the legation bowed. "The señorita will naturally be visited from time to time by an official. Without note—notification. She may be removed whenever His Most Catholic Majesty sees fit. And of course none of her estate will be released before the eighteenth birthday. The whole affair is entirely irregular."

After he left I reproached myself for not asking what Don Jaime's mission had been that fateful evening, or at least for not trying to find out what his function with the Spanish legation was. Probably he could in no way be connected with the counterfeiting of the pesetas. By making no attempt to learn any facts which might have lessened the old feeling of guilty responsibility I kept it uneasily alive.

These reproaches were pushed aside when Catalina put her head against my collarbone, sobbing with relief. "There, there," I said, "there, there."

"Uncouth," reflected Mr Haggerwells. "Compensation indeed!"

"Dealing with natives," said Midbin. "Probably courteous enough to Frenchmen or Afrikanders."

I patted Catalina's quivering shoulders. Child or not, now she was able to talk I had to admit I no longer found her devotion so tiresome. Though I was definitely uneasy lest Barbara discover us in this attitude.

15. GOOD YEARS

*A*ND NOW I come to the period of my life which stands in such sharp contrast to what had gone before. Was it really eight years I spent at Haggershaven? The arithmetic is indisputable: I arrived in 1944 at the age of twenty-three; I left in 1952 at the age of thirty-one. Indisputable, but not quite believable; as with the happy countries which are supposed to have no history I find it hard to go over those eight years and divide them by remarkable events. They blended too smoothly, too contentedly into one another.

Crops were harvested, stored or marketed; the fields were plowed in the fall and again in the spring and sown anew. Three of the older fellows died, another became bedridden. Five new fellows were accepted; two biologists, a chemist, a poet, a philologist. It was to the last I played the same part Ace had to me, introducing him to the sanctuary of the haven, seeing its security and refuge afresh and deeply thankful for the fortune that had brought me to it.

There was no question about success in my chosen profession, not even the expected alternation of achievement and disappointment. Once started on the road I kept on going at an even, steady pace. For what would have been my doctoral thesis I wrote a paper on *The Timing of General Stuart's Maneuvers During August 1863 in Pennsylvania.* This received flattering comment from scholars as far away as the Universities of Lima and Cambridge; because of it I was offered instructorships at highly respectable schools.

I could not think of leaving the haven. The world into which I had been born had never been fully revealed for what it was until I had escaped from it. Secrecy and ugliness; greed, fear and callousness; meanness, avarice, cunning, deceit and self-worship were as close around as the nearest farmhouses. The idea of returning to that world and of entering into daily competition with other underpaid, overdriven drudges striving fruitlessly to apply a dilute coating of culture to the unresponsive surface of unwilling students had little attraction.

In those eight years, as I broadened my knowledge I narrowed my field. Undoubtedly it was presumptuous to take the War of Southron Independence as my specialty when there were already so many comprehensive works on the subject and so many celebrated historians engaged with this special event. However, my choice was made not out of self-importance but fascination, and undoubtedly it was the proximity of the scene which influenced the selection of my goal, the last thirteen months of the war, from General Lee's invasion of Pennsylvania to the capitulation at Reading. I saw the whole vast design: Gettysburg, Lancaster, the siege of Philadelphia, the disastrous Union counter-thrust in Tennessee, the evacuation of Washington, and finally the desperate effort to break out of Lee's trap which ended at Reading. I could spend profitable years filling in the details.

My monographs were published in learned Confederate and British journals—there were none in the United States —and I rejoiced when they brought attention, not so much to me as to Haggershaven. I could contribute only this notice and my physical labor; on the other hand I asked little beyond food, clothing and shelter—just books. My field trips I took on foot, often earning my keep by casual labor for farmers, paying for access to private collections of letters or documents by indexing and arranging them.

The time devoted to scholarship did not alone distinguish those eight years, nor even the security of the haven. I have spoken of the simple, easy manner in which the Agatis admitted me to their friendship, but they were not the only ones with whom there grew ties of affection and understanding. With very few exceptions the fellows of Haggershaven quickly learned to shed the suspicion and aloofness, so necessary a protection elsewhere, and substitute acceptance. The result was a tranquillity I had never experienced before, so that I think of those years as set apart, a golden period, a time of perpetual warm sunshine.

Between Barbara and me the turbulent, ambivalent passion swept back and forth, the periods of estrangement seemingly only a generating force to bring us together again. Hate and love, admiration and distaste, impatience and pity were present on both sides. Only on hers there was jealousy as well; perhaps if I had not been indifferent whenever she chose to respond to some other man she might not have felt the errant desire so strongly. Perhaps not; there was a moral urge behind her behavior. She sneered at women who yielded to such temptations. To her they were not temptations but just rewards; she did not yield, she took them as her due.

Sometimes I wondered if her neurosis did not verge on insanity; I'm sure for her part she must often have stood off and appraised me as a mistake. I know there were many times when I wished there would be no more reconciliation between us.

Yet no amount of thinking could cancel the swift hunger I felt in her presence or the deep mutual satisfaction of physical union. Frequently we were lovers for as long as a month before the inevitable quarrel, followed by varying periods of coolness. During the weeks of distance I remembered how she could be tender and gracious as well as ardent, just as during our intimacy I remembered her ruthlessness and dominance.

It was not only her temperamental outbursts nor even her unappeasable craving for love and affection which thrust us apart. Impediments which, in the beginning, had appeared inconsequential assumed more importance all the time. It was increasingly hard for her to leave her work behind even for moments. She was never allowed to forget, either by her own insatiable drive or by outside acknowledgment that she was already one of the foremost physicists in the world. She had been granted so many honorary degrees she no longer traveled to receive them; offers from foreign governments of well-paid jobs connected with their munitions industries were common. Articles were written about her equation of matter, energy, space and time, acclaiming her as a revolutionary thinker; though she dismissed them as evaluation of elementary work, they nevertheless added to her isolation and curtailed her freedom.

Midbin was, in his way, as much under her spell as Ace or myself. His triumph over Catalina's dumbness he took lightly now it was accomplished; stabilizing Barbara's emotions was the victory he wanted. She, on her side, had lost whatever respect she must have had for him in the days when she had submitted to his treatment. On the very rare occasions when the whim moved her to listen to his entreaties—usually relayed through Ace or me—and grant him time, it seemed to be only for the opportunity of making fun of his efforts. Patiently he tried new techniques of exploration and expression.

"But it's not much use," he said once, dolefully; "she doesnt *want* to be helped."

"Wanting seemed to have little to do with making Catty talk," I pointed out. "Couldnt you . . ."

"Make a tinugraph of Barbara's traumatic shock? If I had the materials there would be no necessity."

Perhaps there was less malice in her mockery now Catty was no longer the focus of his theories about emotional pathology; perhaps she forgave him for her temporary displacement, but she did not withhold her contempt. "Oliver, you should have been a woman," she told him; "you would have been impossible as a mother, but what a grandmother you would have made!"

That Catty herself had in her own way as strong a will as Barbara was demonstrated in her determination to become part of Haggershaven. Her reaction to the visit of the Spanish official was translated into an unyielding program. She had gone resolutely to Thomas Haggerwells, telling him she knew quite well she had neither the aptitudes nor qualifications for admission to fellowship, nor did she ask it. All she wanted was to live in what she regarded as her only home. She would gladly do any work from washing dishes to making clothes—anything she was asked. When she came of age she would turn over whatever money she inherited to the haven without conditions.

He had patiently pointed out that a Spanish subject was a citizen of a far wealthier and more powerful nation than the United States; as an heiress she could enjoy the luxuries and distractions of Madrid or Havana and eventually make a suitable marriage. How silly it would be to give up all these advantages to become an unnoticed, penniless drudge for a group of cranks near York, Pennsylvania.

"He was quite right you know, Catty," I said when she told me about the interview.

She shook her head vigorously, so the loose black curls swirled back and forth. "You think so, Hodge, because you are a hard, prudent Yankee."

I opened my eyes rather wide; this was certainly not the description I would have applied to myself.

"And also because you have Anglo-Saxon chivalry, always rescuing maidens in distress and thinking they must sit on a cushion after that and sew a fine seam. Well, I can sew a fine seam, but sitting on cushions would bore me. Women are not as delicate as you think, Hodge. Nor as terrifying."

Was this last directed toward Barbara? Perhaps Catty had claws. "There's a difference," I said, "between cushion-sitting and living where books and pictures and music are not regarded with suspicion."

"That's right," she agreed; "Haggershaven."

"No, Haggershaven is an anomaly in the United States and in spite of everything it cannot help but be infected by the rest of the country. I meant the great, successful nations who can afford the breathing-spaces for culture."

"But you do not go to them."

"No. This is my country."

"And it will be mine too. After all it was made in the first place by people willing to give up luxuries. Besides you are contradicting yourself: if Haggershaven cannot avoid being infected by what is outside it, neither can any other spot. Part of the world cannot be civilized if another part is backward."

There was no doubt her demure expression hid stern resolution. Whatever else it hid was not so certain. Evidently Mr Haggerwells realized the quality of her determination for eventually he proposed to the fellows that she be allowed to stay and the offer of her money be rejected. The motion was carried, with only Barbara, who spoke long and bitterly against it, voting "no."

In accepting Catty out of charity, the fellows unexpectedly made an advantageous bargain. Not merely because she was always eager to help, but for her specific contribution to the haven's economy. Before this, clothing the haven had been a haphazard affair; suits or dresses were bought with money which would otherwise have been contributed to the general fund, or if the fellow had no outside income, by a grant from the same fund. Catty's artistry with the needle made a revolution. Not only did she patch and mend and alter; she designed and made clothes, conveying some of her enthusiasm to the other women. The haven was better and more handsomely clad and a great deal of money was saved. Only Barbara refused to have her silk trousers and jackets made at home.

It was not entirely easy to adjust to the new Catty, the busy, efficient, selfreliant creature. Her expressive voice could be enchanting even when she was speaking nonsense —and Catty rarely spoke nonsense. I don't mean she was priggish or solemn, quite the contrary; her spontaneous laughter was quick and frequent. But she was essentially not frivolous; she felt deeply, her loyalties were strong and enduring.

I missed her former all too open devotion to me. It had caused embarrassment, impatience, annoyance; now it was withdrawn I felt deprived and even pettish at its lack. Not that I had anything to offer in return or considered that any emotion was called for from me. Though I didnt express it to myself so openly at the time, what I regretted was the sensually valuable docility of a beautiful woman. Of course there was a confusion here: I was regretting what had never been, for Catty and the nameless dumb girl were different individuals. Even her always undeniable beauty was changed and heightened; what I really wanted was for the Catty of now to act like the Catty of then. And without any reciprocal gesture from me.

The new Catty no more than the old was disingenuous or coquettish. She was simply mature, dignified, selfcontained and just a trifle amusedly aloof. Also she was very busy. She did not pretend to any interest in other men; at the same time she had clearly outgrown her childish dependence on me. She refused any competition with Barbara. When I sought her out she was there, but she made no attempt to call me to her.

I was not so unversed that I didnt occasionally suspect this might be a calculated tactic. But when I recalled the utter innocence of her look I reflected I would have to have a very nice conceit of myself indeed to believe the two most attractive women at Haggershaven were contending for me.

I don't know precisely when I began to see Catty with a predatory male eye. Doubtless it was during one of those times when Barbara and I had quarrelled, and when she had called attention to Catty by accusing me of dallying with her. I was essentially as polygamous as Barbara was polyandrous or Catty monogamous; once the idea had formed I made no attempt to reject it.

Nor, for a very long time, did I accept it in any way except academically. There are sensual values also in tantalizing, and if these values are perverse I can only say I was still immature in many ways. Additionally there must have been an element of fear of Catty, the same fear which maintained a reserve against Barbara. For the time being at least it seemed much pleasanter to talk lightly and inconsequentially with her; to laugh and boast of my progress, to discuss Haggershaven and the world, than to face our elementary relationship.

My fourth winter at the haven had been an unusually mild one; spring was early and wet. Kimi Agati who, with her children, annually gathered quantities of mushrooms from the woodlots and pastures, claimed this year's supply was so large that she needed help, and conscripted Catty and me. Catty protested she didnt know a mushroom from a toadstool; Kimi immediately gave her a brief but thorough course in thallophytology. "And Hodge will help you; he's a country boy."

"All right," I said. "I make no guarantees though; I havent been a country boy for a long time."

"I'm not so sure," said Kimi thoughtfully. "You two take the small southeast woodlot; Fumio can have the big pasture, Eiko the small one; Yosh and I will pick in the west woodlot."

We carried a picnic lunch and nests of large baskets which were to be put by the edge of the woodlots when full; late in the afternoon a cart would pick them up and bring them in for drying. The air was warm even under the leafless branches; the damp ground steamed cosily.

"Kimi was certainly right," I commented. "Theyre thick as can be."

"I don't see . . ." She stooped gracefully; "Oh, is this one?"

"Yes," I said, "And there, and there. Not that white thing over there though."

We filled our first baskets without moving more than a few yards. "At this rate we'll have them all full by noon."

"And go back for more?"

"I suppose. Or just wander around."

"Oh . . . Look, Hodge—what's this?"

"What?"

"This." She showed me the puffball in her hands, looking inquiringly up.

I looked down casually; suddenly there was nothing casual between us any more, nor ever would be again. I looked down at a woman I wanted desperately, feverishly, immediately. The shock of desire was a weight on my chest, expelling the air from my lungs.

"Goodness—is it some rare specimen or something?"

"Puffball," I managed to say. "No good."

I hardly spoke, I could hardly speak, as we filled our second baskets. I was sure the pounding of my heart must show through my shirt, and several times I thought I saw her looking curiously at me. "Let's eat now," I suggested hoarsely.

I found a pine with low-hanging boughs and tore down enough to make a dry, soft place to sit while Catty unpacked our picnic. "Here's an egg," she said; "I'm starved."

We ate; that is, she ate and I pretended to. I was half dazed, half terrified. I watched her swift motions, the turn of her head, the clean, sharp way she bit into the food, and averted my eyes every time her glance crossed mine.

"Well," she murmured at last; "I suppose we mustnt sit idle any longer. Come on, lazy; back to work."

"Catty," I whispered. "Catty."

"What is it, Hodge?"

"Wait."

Obediently she paused. I reached over and took her in my arms. She looked at me, not startled, but questioning. Just as my mouth reached hers she moved slightly so that I kissed her cheek instead of her lips. She did not struggle but lay passively, with the same questioning expression.

I held her, pressing her against the pine boughs, and found her mouth. I kissed her eyes and throat and mouth again. Her eyes stayed open and she did not respond. I undid the top of her dress and pressed my face between her breasts.

"Hodge."

I paid no attention.

"Hodge, wait. Listen to me. If this is what you want you know I will not try to stop you. But Hodge, be sure. Be very sure."

"I want you, Catty."

"Do you? Really want *me*, I mean."

"I don't know what you mean. I want you."

But it was already too late; I had made the fatal error of pausing to listen. Angrily I moved away, picked up my basket and sullenly began to search for mushrooms again. My hands still trembled and there was a quiver in my legs. To complement my mood a cloud drifted across the sun and the warm woods became chilly.

"Hodge."

"Yes?"

"Please don't be angry. Or ashamed. If you are I shall be sorry."

"I don't understand."

She laughed. "Oh my dear Hodge. Isnt that what men always say to women? And isnt it always true?"

Suddenly the day was no longer spoiled. The tension melted and we went on picking mushrooms with a new and fresh innocence.

After this I could no longer keep all thoughts of Catty out of the intimacy with Barbara; now for the first time her jealousy had grounds. I felt guilty toward both, not because I desired both, but because I didnt totally desire either.

Now, years later, I condemn myself for the lost rapturous moments; at the time I procrastinated and hesitated as though I had eternity in which to make decisions. I was, as Tyss had said, the spectator type, waiting to be acted upon, waiting for events to push me where they would.

16. OF VARIED SUBJECTS

"*I* CAN'T THINK of anything more futile," said Kimi, "than to be an architect at this time in the United States."

Her husband grinned. "You forgot to add, 'of Oriental extraction.'"

Catty said, "Ive never understood. Of course I don't remember too well, but it seems to me Spanish people don't have the same racial fanaticism. Certainly the Portuguese, French and Dutch don't. Even the English are not quite so certain of Anglo-Saxon superiority. Only the Americans, in the United States and the Confederate States too, judge everything by color."

"The case of the Confederacy is reasonably simple," I said. "There are about fifty million Confederate citizens and two hundred and fifty million subjects. If white supremacy wasnt the cornerstone of Southron policy a visitor couldnt tell the ruling class at a glance. Even as it is he sometimes has a hard time, what with sunburn. It's more complicated here. Remember, we lost a war, the most important war in our history, which was not unconnected with skin color."

"In Japan," said Hiro, "the lighter colored people, the Ainu, used to be looked down on. Just as the Christians were once driven underground at exactly the same time they themselves drove the Jews underground in Spain and Portugal."

"The Jews," murmured Catty vaguely; "are there still Jews?"

142

"Oh yes," I said. "Several millions in Uganda-Eretz which the British made a self-governing dominion back in 1933 under the first Labour cabinet. And numbers most everywhere else, except in the German Union since the massacres of 1905-1913."

"Which were much more thorough than the anti-Oriental massacres in the United States," supplied Hiro.

"Much more thorough," I agreed. "After all, scattered handfuls of Asians were left alive here."

"My parents and Kimi's grandparents among them. How lucky they were to be American Japanese instead of European Jews."

"There are Jews in the United States," announced Kimi. "I met one once. She was a theosophist and told me I ought to learn the wisdom of the East."

"Very few of them. There were about two hundred thousand at the close of the War of Southron Independence on both sides of the border. After the election of 1872, General Grant's Order Number Ten, expelling all Jews from the Department of the Missouri, which had been rescinded immediately by President Lincoln, was retroactively reenacted by President Butler, in spite of the fact that the United States no longer controlled that territory. Henceforth Jews were treated like all other colored peoples, Negroes, Orientals, Indians and South Sea Islanders: as undesirables to be bribed to leave or to be driven out of the country."

"This is very dull stuff," said Hiro. "Let me tell you about a hydrogen reaction—"

"No, please," begged Catty. "Let me listen to Hodge."

"Good heavens," exclaimed Kimi, "when do you ever do anything else? I'd think you'd be tired by now."

"She will marry him one of these days," predicted Hiro; "then the poor fellow will never be allowed to disguise a lecture as a conversation again."

Catty blushed, a deep red blush. I laughed to cover some constraint. Kimi said, "Go-betweens are out of fashion; youre a century behind times, Hiro. I suppose you think a woman ought to walk two paces respectfully behind her husband. Actually, it's only in the United States women can't vote or serve on juries."

"Except in the state of Deseret," I reminded her.

"That's just bait; the Mormons gave us equality because they were running short of women."

"Not the way I heard it. The Latter Day Saints have been the nearest thing to a prosperous group in the country. Women have been moving there for years, it's so easy to get married. All the grumbling about polygamy has come from men who can't stand the competition."

Catty glanced at me, then looked away.

Had she, I wondered afterward, been thinking how Barbara would have rejected my observation furiously? Or about that day in the spring? Or about Hiro's earlier comment? I thought about it, briefly, myself.

I also thought of how easily Catty fitted in with the Agatis and contrasted it with the tension everyone would have felt if Barbara had been there. One could love Barbara, or hate her or dislike her or even, I supposed, be indifferent to her; the one thing impossible was to be comfortable with her.

The final choice (was it final? I don't know. I shall never know now) hardened when I had been nearly six years at Haggershaven. It had been "on" between Barbara and me for the longest stretch I could recall and I had even begun to wonder if some paradoxical equilibrium had not been established which would allow me to be her lover without vexation and at the same time innocently enjoy a bond with Catty.

As always when the hostility between us slackened, Barbara spoke of her work. In spite of such occasional confidences it was still not her habit to talk of it with me. That intimacy was obviously reserved for Ace, and I didnt begrudge him it, for after all he understood what it was all about and I didnt. This time she was so full of the subject she could not hold back, even from one who could hardly distinguish between thermodynamics and kinesthetics.

"Hodge," she said, gray eyes greenish with excitement, "I'm not going to write a book."

"That's nice," I answered idly. "New, too. Saves time,

paper, ink. Sets a different standard; from now on scholars will be known as 'Jones, who didnt write *The Theory of Tidal Waves*', 'Smith, unauthor of *Gas and Its Properties*,' or 'Backmaker, non-recorder of *Gettysburg And After*.' "

"Silly. I only meant it's become customary to spend a lifetime formulating principles; then someone else comes along and puts your principles into practice. It seems more sensible for me to demonstrate my own conclusions instead of writing about them."

"Yes, sure. Youre going to demonstrate . . . uh . . .?"

"Cosmic entity, of course. What do you think Ive been talking about?"

I tried to remember what she had said about cosmic entity. "You mean youre going to try to turn matter into space or something like that?"

"Something like that. I intend to translate matter-energy into terms of space-time."

"Oh," I said, "equations and symbols and all that."

"I just said I wasnt going to write a book."

"But how——" I started up as the impact struck me. "Youre going to . . ." I groped for words. "Youre going to build a . . . an engine which will move through time?"

"Putting it crudely. But close enough for a layman."

"You once told me your work was theoretical. That you were no vulgar mechanic."

"I'll become one."

"Barbara, youre crazy! As a philosophical abstraction this theory of yours is interesting——"

"Thank you. It's always nice to know one has amused the yokelry."

"Barbara, listen to me. Midbin——"

"I havent the faintest interest in Oliver's stodgy fantasies."

"He has in yours though, and so have I. Don't you see, this determination of yours is based on the fantasy of going back through time to——uh——injure your mother——"

"Oliver Midbin is a coarse, stupid, insensate lout. He has taught the dumb to speak, but he's too much of a fool to understand anyone of normal intelligence. He has a set

of idiotic theories about diseased emotions and he fits all
facts into them even if it means chopping them up to do it
or inventing new ones to piece them out. Injure my mother
indeed! I have no more interest in her than she ever had
in me."

"Ah, Barbara—"

" 'Ah Barbara,' " she mimicked. "Run along to your
pompous windbag of a Midbin or your oh-so-willing cow-
eyed Spanish doxy—"

"Barbara, I'm talking as a friend. Leave Midbin and
Catty and personalities out of it and just look at it this
way. Don't you see the difference between promulgating a
theory and trying a practical demonstration which will certainly appear to the world as going over the borderline into
charlatanism? Like a spiritualist medium or—"

"That's enough! 'Charlatan'! You unspeakable gutter-
snipe. What do you know of anything beyond the seduction of cretins? Go back to your trade, you errand boy!"

I seemed to remember that once before an incident had
ended precisely this way. "Barbara—"

Her hand caught me across my mouth. Then she strode
away.

The fellows of Haggershaven were not enthusiastic for
her project. Even as she outlined it to them in more sober
language than she had to me it still sounded outlandish, like
the recurrent idea of a telegraph without wires or a rocket
to the moon. Besides, 1950 was a bad year. The war was
coming closer; at the least, what was left of the independence of the United States was likely to be extinguished. Our
energies had to be directed toward survival rather than new
and expensive ventures. Still, Barbara Haggerwells was a
famous figure commanding great respect, and she had cost
them little so far, beyond paper and pencils. Reluctantly
the fellows voted an appropriation.

An old barn, not utilized for years, but still sound, was
turned over to Barbara, and Kimi was delighted to plan,
design and supervise the necessary changes. Ace and a
group of the fellows attacked the job vigorously, sawing
and hammering, bolting iron beams together, piping in gas

for reflecting lights to enable them to work at night as well.

I believe I took no more interest than was inescapable as a fellow of Haggershaven. I had no doubt that the money and labor were being wasted, and I foresaw a terrible disappointment for Barbara when she realized the impossibility of her project. For myself I did not think she would play any further part of importance in my life.

We had not spoken since the quarrel, nor was there inclination on either side toward coming together again. I could not guess at Barbara's feelings; mine were those of relief, unmixed with regret. I would not have erased all there had been between us, but I was satisfied to have it in the past. The raging desire vanished, gradually replaced by an affection of sorts; I wanted no more of that tempestuous passion, instead I felt aloofly protective and understanding.

For at last I was absorbed with Catty. The raw hunger of the moment when I first realized I wanted her came back with renewed force, but now other, more diffused feelings were equally part of my emotion. I knew she could make me jealous as Barbara could not; at the same time I could see tranquillity beyond turbulent wanting, a tranquillity never possible with Barbara.

But my belated realization of what Catty meant to me was no reaction to Barbara or connected with the breaking of that tie. The need for Catty was engendered by Catty alone, and for Catty apart from anything I had ever felt for another. It was in some ways an entirely new hunger, as the man's need transcends the youth's. I understood now what her question in the woodlot meant and at last I could truthfully answer.

She kissed me back, freely and strongly. "I love you, Hodge," she said; "I have loved you even through the bad dream of not being able to speak."

"When I was so unfeeling."

"I loved you even when you were impatient; I tried to make myself prettier for you. You know you have never said I was pretty."

"You arent, Catty. Youre extraordinarily beautiful."

"I think I would rather be pretty. Beauty sounds forbidding. Oh, Hodge if I did not love you so much I would not have stopped you that day."

"I'm not sure I understand that."

"No? Well, it is not necessary now. Sometimes I wondered if I had been right after all, or if you would think it was because of Barbara."

"Wasnt it?"

"No. I was never jealous of her. We Garcías are supposed to have Morisco blood; perhaps I have the harem outlook of my dark Muslim ancestors. Would you like me to be your black concubine?"

"No," I said. "I'd like you to be my wife. In any colors you have."

"Spoken with real gallantry; you will be a courtier yet, Hodge. But that was a proposal, wasnt it?"

"Yes," I answered grimly; "if you will consider one from me. I can't think of any good reason why you should."

She put her hands on my shoulders and looked into my eyes. "I don't know what reason has to do with it. It is what I always intended; that was why I blushed so when Hiro Agati blurted out what everyone could see."

Later I said, "Catty, can you ever forgive me for the wasted years? You say you werent jealous of Barbara, but surely if she and I—that is . . . anyway, forgive me."

"Dear Hodge, there's nothing to forgive. Love is not a business transaction, nor a case at law in which justice is sought, nor a reward for having good qualities. I understand you, Hodge, better I think than you understand yourself. You are not satisfied with what is readily obtained, otherwise you would have been content back in—what is the name?—Wappinger Falls. I have known this for a long time and I could, I think—you must excuse my vanity—have interested you at any moment by pretending fickleness. Just as I could have held you if I had given in that day. Besides, I think you will make a better husband for realizing you could not deal with Barbara."

I can't say I entirely enjoyed this speech. I felt, in fact, rather humiliated, or at least healthily humbled. Which was no doubt what she intended, and as it should be. I never had the idea she was frail or insipid.

Nor did Catty's explanation of a harem outlook satisfactorily account for the sudden friendliness of the two women after the engagement was announced. That Barbara should soften so toward a successful rival was incomprehensible and also disturbing.

Because both were fully occupied they actually spent little time together, but Catty visited the workshop, as they called the converted barn, whenever she had the chance and her real admiration for Barbara grew so that I heard too often of her genius, courage and imagination. I could hardly ask Catty to forego society I had so recently found enchanting nor establish a taboo against mention of a name I had lately whispered with ardor; still I felt a little foolish, and not quite as important as I might otherwise have thought myself.

Not that Catty didnt have proper respect and enthusiasm for my fortunes. I had completed my notes for *Chancellorsville to the End*—that is, I had a mass of clues, guideposts, keys, ideas, and emphases which would serve as skeleton for a work which might take years to write—and Catty was the audience to whom I explained and expounded and used as a prototype of the reader I might reach. Volume one was roughly drafted, and we were to be married as soon as it was finished, shortly after my thirtieth and Catty's twenty-fourth birthday. There was little doubt the book would bring an offer from one of the great Confederate universities, but Catty was firm for a cottage like the Agatis', and I could not conceive of being foolish enough to leave Haggershaven.

From Catty's talk I knew Barbara was running into increasing difficulties now the workshop was complete and actual construction begun of what was referred to, with unnecessary crypticism I thought, as HX-1. The impending war created scarcities, particularly of such materials as steel and copper, of which latter metal HX-1 seemed inordinately greedy. I was not surprised when the fellows apologetically refused Barbara a new appropriation.

Next day Catty said, "Hodge, you know the haven wouldnt take my money."

"And quite right too. Let the rest of us put in what we get; we owe it to the haven anyway. But the debt is the other way round in your case and you should keep your independence."

"Hodge, I'm going to give it all to Barbara for her HX-1."

"What? Oh, nonsense!"

"Is it any more nonsensical for me to put in money I didnt do anything to get than for her and Ace to put in time and knowledge and labor?"

"Yes, because she's got a crazy idea and Ace has never been quite sane where she's concerned. If you go ahead and do this you'll be as crazy as they are."

When Catty laughed I remembered with a pang the long months when that lovely sound had been strangled by terror inside her. I also thought with shame of my own failure; had I appreciated her when her need was greatest I might have eased the long, painful ordeal of restoring her voice.

"Perhaps I am crazy. Do you think the haven would make me a fellow on that basis? Anyway, I believe in Barbara even if the rest of you don't. Not that I'm criticizing; you were right to be cautious. You have more to consider than demonstration of the truth of a theory which can't conceivably have a material value; I don't have to take any such long view. Anyway I believe in her. Or perhaps I feel I owe her something. With my money she can finish her project. I only tell you this because you may not want to marry me under the circumstances."

"You think I'm marrying you for your money?"

She smiled. "Dear Hodge. You are in some ways so young; I hear the wounded dignity in your voice. No, I know very well you arent marrying me for money, that it never occurred to you it might be a good idea. That would be too practical, too grown up, too un-Hodgelike. I think you might not want to marry a woman who'd give all her money away. Especially to Barbara Haggerwells."

"Catty, are you doing this absurd thing to get rid of me? Or to test me?"

This time she again laughed loud. "Now I'm sure you will marry me after all and turn out to be a puzzled but amenable husband. You are my true Hodge, who studies a war because he can't understand anything simpler or subtler."

She wasnt to be dissuaded from the quixotic gesture. I might not understand subtleties but I was sure I understood Barbara well enough. Foreseeing her request for more funds would be turned down, she must have cultivated Catty deliberately in order to use her. Now she'd gotten what she wanted I confidently expected her to drop Catty or revert to her accustomed virulence.

She did neither. If anything the amity grew. Catty's vocabulary added words like "magnet," "coil," "induction," "particle," "light-year," "continuum" and many others either incomprehensible or uninteresting to me. Breathlessly she described the strange, asymmetric structure taking shape in the workshop, while my mind was busy with Ewell's Corps and parrott guns and the weather chart of southern Pennsylvania for July, 1863.

The great publishing firm of Ticknor, Harcourt & Knopf contracted for my book—there was no publisher in the United States equipped to handle it—and sent me a sizable advance in Confederate dollars which became even more sizable converted into our money. I read the proofs of volume one in a state of semiconsciousness, sent the inevitable telegram changing a footnote on page 99, and waited for the infuriating mails to bring me my complimentary copies. The day after they arrived (with a horrifying typographical error right in the middle of page 12), Catty and I were married.

Dear Catty. Dear, dear Catty.

With the approval of the fellows we used part of the publisher's advance for a honeymoon. We spent it—that part of it in which we had time for anything except being alone together—going over nearby battlefields of the last year of the War of Southron Independence.

It was Catty's first excursion away from Haggershaven
since the night I brought her there. Looking at the world
outside through her perceptions, at once insulated and
made hypersensitive by her new status, I was shocked
afresh at the harsh indifference, the dull poverty, the fear,
brutality, frenzy and cynicism highlighting the strange resignation to impending fate which characterized our civilization. It was not a case of eat, drink, be merry, for tomorrow we die; rather it was, let us live meanly and trust
to luck—tomorrow's luck is bound to be worse.

We settled down in the autumn of 1951 in a cottage
designed by Kimi and built by the fellows during our absence. It gave on the Agatis' cherished garden and we were
both moved by this evidence of love, particularly after
what we had seen and heard on our trip. Mr Haggerwells
made a speech, filled with classical allusions, welcoming
us back as though we had been gone for years; Midbin
looked anxiously into Catty's face as though to assure himself I had not, in my new role as husband, treated her so ill
as to bring on a new emotional upset; and the other fellows made appropriate gestures. Even Barbara stopped by
long enough to comment that the house was ridiculously
small, but she supposed Kimi's movable partitions helped.

I immediately began working on volume two and Catty
took up her sewing again. She also resumed her visits to
Barbara's workshop; again I heard detailed accounts of
my former sweetheart's progress. HX-1 was to be completed in the late spring, or early summer. I was not surprised at Barbara's faith surviving actual construction of
the thing, but that such otherwise level-headed people as
Ace and Catty could envisage breathlessly the miracles
about to happen was beyond me. Ace, even after all these
years, was still bemused—but Catty . . . ?

Just before the turn of the year I got the following letter:

LEE & WASHINGTON UNIVERSITY
Department of History

Leesburg, District of Calhounia, CSA.
December 19, 1951

Mr. Hodgins M. Backmaker
"Haggershaven"
York,
Pennsylvania, USA.

Sir:

On page 407 of Chancellorsville to the End, *volume 1,* Turning Tides, *you write, "Chronology and topography—timing and the use of space—were to be the decisive factors, rather than population and industry. Stuart's detachment, which might have proved disastrous, turned out extraordinarily fortunate for Lee, as we shall see in the next volume. Of course the absence of cavalry might have been decisive if the Round Tops had not been occupied by the Southrons on July 1 . . ."*

Now, sir, evidently in your forthcoming analysis of Gettysburg you hold (as I presume most Yankees do) to the theory of fortuitousness. We Southrons naturally ascribe the victory to the supreme genius of General Lee, regarding the factors of time and space not as forces in themselves but as opportunities for the display of his talents.

Needless to say, I hardly expect you to change your opinions, rooted as they must be in national pride. I only ask that before you commit them, and the conclusions shaped by them, to print, you satisfy yourself as an historian, of their validity in this particular case. In other words, sir, as one of your readers (and may I add, one who has enjoyed your work), I should like

*to be assured that you have studied this classic battle
as carefully as you have the engagements described in
volume I.*

> *With earnest wishes for your success,
> I remain, sir
> Cordially yours,
>   Jefferson Davis Polk*

This letter from Dr Polk, the foremost historian of our
day, author of the monumental biography, *The Great Lee,*
produced a crisis in my life. Had the Confederate professor pointed out flaws in my work, or even reproached me
for undertaking it at all without adequate equipment I
would, I trust, have acknowledged the reproof and continued to the best of my ability. But this letter was an acco-
lade. Without condescension Dr Polk admitted me to the
ranks of serious historians, only asking me to consider the
depth of my evaluation.

Truth is, I was not without increasing doubts of my own.
Doubts I had not allowed to rise to the surface of my mind
and disturb my plans. Polk's letter brought them into the
open.

I had read everything available. I had been over the
ground between the Maryland line, South Mountain, Car-
lisle and the haven until I could draw a detail map from
memory. I had turned up diaries, letters and accounts
which had not only never been published, but which were
not known to exist until I hunted them down. I had so
steeped myself in the period I was writing about that sometimes the two worlds seemed interchangeable and I could
live partly in one, partly in the other.

Yet with all this, I was not sure I had the whole story,
even in the sense of wholeness that historians, knowing
they can never collect every detail, accept. I was not sure
I had the grand scene in perfectly proper perspective. I admitted to myself the possibility that I had perhaps been
too rash, too precipitate, in undertaking *Chancellorsville to
the End* so soon. I knew the shadowy sign, the one which

says in effect, *You are ready*, had not been given. My confidence was shaken.

Was the fault in me, in my temperament and character, rather than in my preparation and use of materials? Was I drawing back from committing myself, from acting, from doing? That I had written the first volume was no positive answer, for it was but the fraction of a whole deed; if I withdrew now I could still preserve my standing as an onlooker.

But not to act was itself an action and answered neither Dr Polk nor myself. Besides, what could I do? The entire work was contracted for. The second volume was promised for delivery some eighteen months hence. My notes for it were complete; this was no question of revising, but of wholly re-examining, revaluing and probably discarding them for an entirely new start. It was a job so much bigger than the original, one so discouraging, I felt I couldnt face it. It would be corrupt to produce a work lacking absolute conviction and cowardly to produce none.

Catty responded to my awkward recapitulation in a way at once heartening and strange. "Hodge," she said, "youre changing and developing, and for the better, even though I love you as you were. Don't be afraid to put the book aside for a year—ten years if you have to. You must do it so it will satisfy yourself; never mind what the publishers or the public say. But Hodge, you mustnt, in your anxiety, or your foolish fear of passiveness, you mustnt try any shortcuts. Promise me that."

"I don't know what youre talking about, Catty dear. There are no shortcuts in writing history."

She looked at me thoughtfully. "Remember that, Hodge. Oh, remember it."

17. HX-1

I COULD NOT bring myself to follow the promptings of my conscience and Catty's advice, nor could I use my notes as though Dr Polk's letter had never come to shatter my complacency. As a consequence—without deliberately committing myself to abandon the book—I worked not at all, thus adding to my feelings of guilt and unworthiness. The tasks assigned by the fellows for the general welfare of the haven were not designed to take a major part of my time, and though I produced all sorts of revolutions in the stables and barns, I still managed to wander about, fretful and irritable, keeping Catty from her work, interrupting the Agatis and Midbin—I could not bring myself to discuss my problems with him—and generally making myself a nuisance. Inevitably I found my way into Barbara's workshop.

She and Ace had done a thorough job on the old barn. I thought I recognized Kimi's touch in the structural changes of the walls, the strong beams and rows of slanted-in windows which admitted light and shut out glare, but the rest must have been shaped by Barbara's needs.

Iron beams held up a catwalk running in a circle about ten feet overhead. On the catwalk there were at intervals what appeared to be batteries of telescopes, all pointed inward and downward at the center of the floor. Just inside the columns was a continuous ring of clear glass, perhaps four inches in diameter, fastened to the beams with glass hooks. Closer inspection proved the ring not to be in one piece but in sections, ingeniously held together with glass couplings. Back from this circle, around the walls, were various engines, all enclosed except for dial faces and regulators and all dwarfed by a mammoth one towering in one corner. From the roof was suspended a large, polished reflector.

There was no one in the barn and I wandered about, cautiously avoiding the mysterious apparatus. For a moment I meditated, basely perhaps, that all this had been paid for with my wife's money. Then I berated myself, for Catty owed all to the haven, as I did. The money might have been put to better use, but there was no guarantee it would have been more productive allotted to astronomy or zoology. During eight years I'd seen many promising schemes come to nothing.

"Like it, Hodge?"

Barbara had come up, unheard, behind me. This was the first time we had been alone together since our break, two years before.

"It looks like a tremendous amount of work," I evaded.

"It was a tremendous amount of work." For the first time I noticed that her cheeks were flushed. She had lost weight and there were deep hollows beneath her eyes. "This construction has been the least of it. Now it's done. Or has begun. Depending how you look at it."

"All done?"

She nodded, triumph accenting the strained look on her face. "First test today."

"Oh well . . . in that case—"

"Don't go, Hodge. Please. I meant to ask you and Catty to the more formal trial, but now youre here for the preliminary I'm glad. Ace and Father and Oliver will be along in a minute."

"Midbin?"

The familiar arrogance showed briefly. "I insisted. It'll be nice to show him the mind can produce something besides fantasies and hysterical hallucinations."

I started to speak, then swallowed my words. The dig at Catty was insignificant compared with the supreme confidence, the abnormal assurance prompting invitations to witness a test which could only reveal the impossibility of applying her cherished theories. I felt an overwhelming pity. "Surely," I said at last, seeking to make some preparation for the disillusionment certain to come, "surely you don't expect it to work the first time?"

"Why not? There are sure to be adjustments to be made, allowances for erratic chronology caused by phenomena like the pull of comets and so forth. There might even have to be major alterations, though I doubt it. It may be some time before Ace can set me down at the exact year, month, day, hour and minute agreed upon. But the fact of space-time-energy-matter correspondence can just as well be established this afternoon as next year."

She was unbelievably at ease for someone whose lifework was about to be weighed. I have shown more nervousness discussing a disputed date with the honorary secretary of a local historical society.

"Sit down," she invited; "there's nothing to do or see till Ace comes. Ive missed you, Hodge."

I felt this was a dangerous remark, and wished I'd stayed far away from the workshop. I hooked my leg over a stool —there were no chairs—and coughed to hide the fact I was afraid to answer, Ive missed you too; and afraid not to.

"Tell me about your own work, Hodge. Catty says youre having difficulties."

I was faintly annoyed with Catty, but whether for confiding in Barbara at all or specifically for revealing something unheroic, I didnt stop to consider. At any rate this annoyance diluted my feeling of disloyalty for conversing with Barbara at all. Or it may be the old, long-established bond—I almost wrote, of sympathy, but it was so much more complex than the word indicates—was reawakened by proximity and put me in the mood to tell my troubles. It is even possible I had the altruistic purpose of fortifying Barbara against inevitable disappointment on a misery-loves-company basis. Be that as it may, I found myself pouring out the whole story.

She jumped up and took my hands in hers. Her eyes were gray and warm. "Hodge! It's wonderful—don't you see?"

"Oh ..." I was completely confused. "I ... uh ..."

"The solution. The answer. The means. Look: now you can go back, back to the past in your own person. You can see everything with your own eyes instead of relying on accounts of what other people said happened."

"But . . . but—"

"You can verify every fact, study every move, every actor. You can write history as no one ever did before, for youll be writing as a witness, yet with the perspective of a different period. Youll be taking the mind of the present, with its judgment and its knowledge of the patterns, back to receive the impressions of the past. It almost seems HX-1 was devised especially for this."

There was no doubt she believed, that she was really and unselfishly glad her work could aid mine. I was overcome by pity, helpless to soften the disillusionment so soon to come and filled with an irrational hatred of the thing she had built and which was about to destroy her.

I was saved from having to mask my emotions by the arrival of her father, Ace, and Midbin. Thomas Haggerwells began tensely, "Barbara, Ace tells me you intend to try out this—this machine on yourself. I can't believe you would be so foolhardy."

Midbin didnt wait for her to reply. I thought with something of a shock, Midbin has gotten old; I never noticed it. "Listen to me. There's no point now in saying part of your mind realizes the impossibility of this demonstration and that it's willing for you to annihilate yourself in the attempt and so escape from conflicts which have no resolution. Although it's something you must be at least partly aware of. But consider objectively the danger involved in meddling with unknown natural laws—"

Ace Dorn, who looked as strained as they in contrast to Barbara's ease, growled, "Let's go."

She smiled reassuringly at us. "Please, Father, don't worry; there's no danger. And Oliver . . ."

Her smile was almost mischievous and very unlike the Barbara I had known. "Oliver, HX-1 owes more to you than you will ever know."

She ducked under the transparent ring and walked to the center of the floor, glancing up at the reflector, moving an inch or two to stand directly beneath it. "The controls are already adjusted to minus fifty-two years and a hundred and fifty-three days," she informed us conversationally. "Purely arbitrary. One date is good as another, but January 1, 1900 is an almost automatic choice. I'll be gone sixty seconds. Ready, Ace?"

"Ready." He had been slowly circling the engines, checking the dials. He took his place before the largest, the monster in the corner, holding a watch in his hand. "Three forty-three and ten," he announced.

Barbara was consulting her own watch. "Three forty-three and ten," she confirmed. "Make it at three forty-three and twenty."

"OK. Good luck."

"You might at least try it on an animal first," burst out Midbin, as Ace twirled the valve under his hand. The transparent ring glowed, the metal reflector threw back a dazzling light. I blinked. When I opened my eyes the light was gone and the center of the workshop was empty.

No one moved. Ace frowned over his watch. I stared at the spot where Barbara had stood. I don't think my mind was working; I had the feeling my lungs and heart certainly were not. I was a true spectator, with all faculties save sight and hearing suspended.

". . . on an animal first." Midbin's voice was querulous.

"Oh, God . . ." muttered Thomas Haggerwells.

Ace said casually—too casually, "The return is automatic. Set beforehand for duration. Thirty more seconds."

Midbin said, "She is . . . this is . . ." He sat down on a stool and bent his head almost to his knees.

Mr Haggerwells groaned, "Ace, Ace—you should have stopped her."

"Ten seconds," said Ace firmly.

Still I couldnt think with any clarity. She had stood there; then she was gone. What . . .? Midbin was right: we had let her go to destruction. Certainly more than a minute had passed by now.

The ring glowed and the brilliant light was reflected. "It did, oh, it did!" Barbara cried. "It did!"

She stood perfectly still, overwhelmed. Then she came

out of the circle and kissed Ace, who patted her gently on the back. I suddenly noticed the pain of holding my breath and released a tremendous sigh. Barbara kissed her father and Midbin—who was still shaking his head—and, after the faintest hesitation, me. Her lips were ice-cold.

The shock of triumph made her voluble. Striding up and down, she spoke with extraordinary rapidity, without pause, almost a little drunkenly. In her excitement her words cluttered her tongue; from time to time she had to go back and repeat a phrase or sentence to make it intelligible.

When the light flashed, she too involuntarily closed her eyes. She had felt a strange, terrifying weightlessness, an awful disembodiment, for which she had been unprepared. She thought she had not actually been unconscious, even for an instant, though she had an impression of ceasing to exist as a unique collection of memories, and of being somehow dissolved. Then she had opened her eyes.

At first she was shocked to find the barn as it had been all her life, abandoned and dusty. Then she realized she had indeed moved through time; the disappearance of the engines and reflector showed she had gone back to the unremodelled workshop.

Now she saw the barn was not quite as she had known it, even in her childhood, for while it was unquestionably abandoned, it had evidently not long been so. The thick dust was not so thick as she remembered, the sagging cobwebs not so dense. Straw was still scattered on the floor; it had not yet been entirely carried away by mice or inquisitive birds. Alongside the door hung bits of harness beyond repair, some broken bridles, and a faded calendar on which the ink of the numerals 1897 was still bright.

The minute she had allotted this first voyage seemed fantastically short and incredibly long. All the paradoxes she had brushed aside as of no immediate concern now confronted her. Since she had gone back to a time before she was born, she must have existed as a visitor prior to her own conception; she could presumably be present during her own childhood and growth, and by making a second and third visit, multiply herself as though in facing mirrors, so that an infinite number of Barbara Haggerwells could occupy a single segment of time.

A hundred other parallel speculations raced through her mind without interfering with her rapid and insatiable survey of the commonplace features of the barn, features which could never really be commonplace to her since they proved all her speculations so victoriously right.

Suddenly she shivered with the bitter cold and burst into teeth-chattering laughter. She had made such careful plans to visit on the First of January—and had never thought to take along a warm coat.

She looked at her watch; only twenty seconds had passed. The temptation to defy her agreement with Ace not to step outside the tiny circle of HX-1's operating field on the initial experiment was almost irresistible. She longed to touch the fabric of the past, to feel the worn boards of the barn, to handle as well as look. Again her thoughts whirled with speculation; again the petty moment stretched and contracted. She spent eternity and instantaneity at once.

Suppose . . . But she had a thousand suppositions and questions. Was she really herself in the flesh, or in some mental projection? A pinch would do no good; that might be projection also. Would she be visible to the people of the time, or was she a ghost from the future? Oh, there was so much to learn, so much to encounter!

When the moment of return came, she again experienced the feeling of dissolution, followed immediately by the light. When she opened her eyes she was back.

Midbin rubbed his belly and then his thinning hair. "Hallucination," he propounded at last; "a logical, consistent hallucination. Answer to an overriding wish."

"You mean Barbara was never gone?" asked Ace. "Was she visible to you—or Mr H or Hodge—during that minute?"

"Illusion," said Midbin; "group illusion brought on by suggestion and anxiety."

"Nonsense," exclaimed Barbara. "Unless youre accusing Ace and me of faking youll have to account for what you just called the logical consistency of it. Your group illusion and my individual hallucination fitting so neatly together."

Midbin recovered some of his poise. "The two phenomena are separate, connected only by some sort of emotional hypnosis. Certainly your daydream of having been back in 1900 is an emotionally induced aberration."

"And your daydream that I wasnt here for a minute?"

"The eyes are quickly affected by the feelings. Note tears, 'seeing red' and so forth."

"Very well, Oliver. The only thing to do is to let you try HX-1 yourself."

"Hay, my turn's supposed to be next," protested Ace.

"Of course. But no one is going to use it again today. Tomorrow morning. Bring Catty, Hodge, if she wants to come, but please don't say anything to anyone else till weve made further demonstrations, otherwise we'll be besieged by fellows wanting to take short jaunts into popular years."

I had little inclination to discuss what had happened with anyone, even Catty. Not that I shared Midbin's theory of nothing material having taken place; I knew I'd not seen Barbara for sixty seconds and I was convinced her account of them was accurate. What confused me was the shock to my preconceptions involved in her proof. If time and space, matter and energy were the same, as fog and ice and water are the same, then I—the physical I at least—and Catty, the world and the universe must be, as Enfandin had insisted, mere illusion. In that sense Midbin had been right.

I went furtively to the workshop next day without telling Catty, as though we were all engaged in some dark necromancy, some sacrilegious rite. Apparently I was the only one who had spent an anxious night; Mr Haggerwells looked proud, Barbara looked satisfied, Ace cocky, and even Midbin, for no understandable reason, benign.

"All here?" inquired Ace. "I'm eager as a fox in a henhouse. Three minutes in 1885. Why 1885? I don't know; a year when nothing much happened, I suppose. Ready, Barbara?"

He returned to report he had found the barn well occupied by both cattle and fowl, and been scared stiff of discovery when the dogs set up a furious barking.

"That pretty well settles the question of corporeal presence," I remarked.

"Not at all," said Mr Haggerwells unexpectedly. "Dogs are notoriously psychic."

"Ah," cried Ace, bringing his hands from behind his back; "look at this. I could hardly have picked it up with psychic feelers."

"This" was a newlaid egg, sixty-seven years old. Or was it? Trips in time are confusing that way.

Barbara was upset, more than I thought warranted. "Oh, Ace, how could you be so foolish? We darent be anything but spectators, as unseen as possible."

"Why? Ive a notion to court my grandmother and wind up as my own grandfather."

"Don't be stupid. The faintest indication of our presence, the slightest impingement on the past, may change the whole course of events. We have no way of knowing what actions have no consequences—if there can be any. Goodness knows what your idiocy with the egg has done. It's absolutely essential not to betray ourselves in any way. Please remember this in future."

"You mean, 'Remember this in past,' don't you?"

"Ace, this isnt a joke."

"It isn't a wake either. I can't see the harm in bringing back tangible proof. Loss of one egg isnt going to send the prices up for 1885 and cause retroactive inflation. Youre making a mountain out of a molehill—or an omelette out of a single egg."

She shrugged helplessly. "Oliver, I hope you won't be so foolish."

"Since I don't expect to arrive in, say, 1820, I can safely promise neither to steal eggs nor court Ace's female ancestors."

He was gone for five minutes. The barn had apparently not yet been built in 1820 and he found himself on a slight rise in a field of wild hay. The faint snick of scythes, and voices not too far off, indicated mowers. He dropped to the ground. His view of the past was restricted to tall grass and some persistent ants who explored his face and hands until the time was up and he returned with broken spears of ripe hay clinging to his clothes.

"At least that's what I imagined I saw," he concluded.

"Did you imagine these?" asked Ace, pointing to the straws.

"Probably. It's at least as likely as time-travel."

"But what about corroboration? Your experience, and Barbara's and Ace's confirm each other. Doesnt that mean anything?"

"Certainly. Only I'm not prepared to say what. The mind can do anything; anything at all. Create boils and cancers. Why not ants and grass? I don't know. I don't know . . ."

After more fruitless argument, he and I left the workshop. I was again reminded of Enfandin—Why should I believe my eyes? I felt though that Midbin was carrying skepticism beyond rational limits; Barbara's case was proved.

"Yes, yes," he answered when I said this. "Why not?"

I puzzled over his reply. Then he added abruptly, "No one can help her now."

18. THE WOMAN TEMPTED ME

*G*ENTLY, Catty said, "Ive never understood why you cut yourself off from the past the way you have, Hodge."

"Ay? What do you mean?"

"Well, youve not communicated with your father or mother since you left home, fourteen years ago. You say you had a dear friend in the man from Haiti, yet youve never tried to find out whether he lived or died."

"Oh, that way. I thought you meant . . . something different." By not taking advantage of Barbara's offer I certainly was cutting myself off from the past.

"Yes?"

"Well, I guess more or less everyone at the haven has done the same thing. Let outside ties grow weak, I mean. You for one—"

"But I have no parents, no friends anywhere else. All my life is here."

"Well, so is mine."

"Ah, dear Hodge; it is unlike you to be so indifferent."

"Catty darling, you were brought up comfortably in an atmosphere knowing nothing of indenting or sharecropping, of realizing the only escape from wretchedness was in a miracle—usually translated as a winning number in the lottery. I can't convey to you the meaning of utterly loveless surroundings, I can only say that affection was a luxury my mother and father couldnt afford."

"Perhaps not; but you can afford it. Now. And nothing of what you have said applies to Enfandin."

I squirmed shamefacedly. My ingratitude and callousness must be apparent to everyone; even Barbara, I remembered, had once asked me much the same questions Catty asked now. How could I explain, even to my own satisfaction, how procrastination and guilt made it impossible for me to take the simple steps to discover what had happened to my friend? By a tremendous effort I might have broken through the inertia years ago, just after Enfandin had been wounded, but each day and month between confirmed the impossibility more strongly. "Let the past take care of itself," I muttered.

"Oh Hodge! What a thing for an historian to say."

"Catty, I can't."

The conversation made me nervous and fidgetty. It also made me remember much I preferred to let fade: the Grand Army, Sprovis, the counterfeit pesetas . . . All the evil I had unwillingly abetted. If a man did nothing, literally nothing, all his life, then he might be free of culpability. Manichaeism, said Enfandin. No absolution.

My idleness, I knew very well, heightened all these feelings of degradation. Were I able to continue in the happy, cocksure way I had gone about my note-gathering and the writing of volume one, I would have neither the time nor susceptibility to be plagued by this disquiet. As it was I seemed to be able to do nothing but act as audience for what was going on in the workshop.

With childish eagerness Barbara and Ace explored HX-1's possibilities for the next two months. They quickly learned that its range was limited to little more than a century, though this limit was subject to slight variations. When they tried to operate beyond this range the translation simply didnt take place, though the same feeling of dissolution occurred. When the light faded they were still in the present. Midbin's venture into the hayfield had been a freak, possibly due to peculiar weather conditions at both ends of the journey. They set 1850 as a safe limit, with an undefined marginal zone further back which was not to be hazarded lest conditions change during the journey and the traveler be lost.

Why this limit existed at all was a matter of dispute between them, a dispute of which I must admit I understood little. Barbara spoke of subjective factors which seemed to mean that HX-1 worked slightly differently in the case of each person it transported; Ace of magnetic fields and power relays, which didnt mean anything to me at all. The only thing they agreed on was that the barrier was not immutable; HX-2 or 3 or 20, if they were ever built, would undoubtedly overcome it.

Nor would HX-1 work in reverse; the future remained closed, probably for similar reasons, whatever they were. Here again they disputed, Ace holding an HX could be built for this purpose, Barbara insisting that new equations would have to be worked out.

They confirmed their tentative theory that time spent in the past consumed an equal amount of time in the present; they could not return to a point a minute after departure when they had been gone for an hour. As near as I could understand, this was because duration was set in the present. In order to come back to a time-point not in correspondence with the period actually spent, another HX, or at least another set of controls, would have to be taken into the past. And then they would not work since HX-1 could not penetrate the future.

The most inconvenient circumscription was the inability of one person to visit the same past moment twice. When the attempt was made the feeling of dissolution did not occur, the light went on and off with no effect upon the would-be traveler standing beneath it. Here Barbara's "subjective factor" was triumphant, but why, or how it worked, they did not know. Nor did they know what would happen to a traveler who attempted to overlap by being already on the spot prior to a previous visit; it was too dangerous to try.

Within these limits they roamed almost at will. Ace spent a full week in October 1896, walking as far as Philadelphia, enjoying the enthusiasm and fury of the presidential campaign. Knowing President Bryan was not only going to be elected, but would serve three terms, he found it hard indeed to obey Barbara's stricture and not cover confident Whig bets on Major McKinley.

Though both sampled the war years they brought back

nothing useful to me, no information or viewpoint I couldnt have got from any of a score of books. Lacking historians' interests or training, their tidbits were those of curious onlookers, not probing chroniclers. It was tantalizing to know that Barbara had seen Secretary Stanton at the York depot or that Ace had overheard a farmer say casually that Southron scouts had stopped at his place the day before and they had thought neither incident worth investigating further.

I grew increasingly fretful. I held long colloquies with myself which always ended inconclusively. *Why not?* I asked. *Surely this is the unique opportunity. Never before has it been possible for an historian to check back at will, to select a particular moment for personal scrutiny, to write of the past with the detachment of the present and the accuracy of an eyewitness knowing specifically what to look for. Why don't you take advantage of HX-1 and see for yourself?*

Against this I objected—what? Fear? Uneasiness? The "subjective factor" in HX-1? The superstitious notion that I might be tampering with a taboo, with matters forbidden to human shortcomings? *You mustnt try any shortcuts. Promise me that, Hodge.* Well, Catty was a darling. She was my beloved wife, but she was neither scholar nor oracle. On what grounds did she protest? Woman's intuition? A respectable phrase, but what did it mean? And didnt Barbara, who first suggested my using HX-1, have womanly intuition also?

A half-dozen times I tried to steer our talk in the direction of my thoughts; each time I allowed the words to drift to another topic. What was the use of upsetting her? *Promise me that, Hodge.* But I had not promised. This was something I had to settle for myself.

What was I afraid of? Because I'd never grasped anything to do with the physical sciences did I attribute some anthropomorphism to their manifestations and like a savage fear the spirit imprisoned in what I didnt understand? (But HX-1 *did* have subjective factors.) I had never thought of myself as hidebound, but I was acting like a ninety-year-old professor asked to use a typewriter instead of a goose quill.

I recalled Tyss's, "You are the spectator type, Hodgins." And once I had called him out of my memory I couldnt escape his familiar, sardonic, interminable argument. *Why are you fussing yourself, Hodgins? What is the point of all this introspective debate? Don't you know your choice has already been made? And that you have acted according to it an infinite number of times and will do so an infinite number of times again? Relax, Hodgins; you have nothing to worry about. Free will is an illusion; you cannot alter what you are about to decide under the impression that you have decided.*

My reaction to this imagined interjection was frenzied, unreasonable. I cursed Tyss and his damnable philosophy. I cursed the insidiousness of his reasoning which had planted seed in my brain to sprout at a moment like this.

Yet in spite of the violence of my rejection of the words I attributed to Tyss, I accepted one of them. I relaxed. The decision had been made. Not by mechanistic forces, nor by blind response to stimulus, but by my own desire.

And now to my aid came the image of Tyss's antithesis, René Enfandin. *Be a skeptic, Hodge; be always the skeptic. Prove all things; hold fast to that which is true. Joking Pilate, asking,* What is truth? *was blind. But you can see more aspects of the absolute truth than any man has had a chance to see before. Can you use the chance well, Hodge? That is the only question.*

Once I could answer it with a vigorous affirmative, and so buttress the determination to go, I was faced with the problem of telling Catty. I could not shut her out of so important a move. I told myself I could not bear the thought of her anxiety; that she would worry despite the fact others had frequently used HX-1, for my object could not be accomplished in a matter of minutes or hours. I was sure she would be sick with apprehension during the days I would be gone. No doubt this was all true, but I also remembered, *Promise me, Hodge . . .*

I finally took the weak, the ineffective course. I said I'd decided the only way to face my problem was to go to

Gettysburg and spend three or four days going over the actual field. Here, I explained unconvincingly, I thought I might at last come to the conclusion whether to scrap all my work and start afresh, or not.

Her faintly oblique eyes were inscrutable. She pretended to believe me and begged me to take her along. After all, we had spent our honeymoon on battlefields.

Would it be possible? Two people had never stood under the reflector together, but surely it would work? I was tempted, but I could not subject Catty to the risk, however slight. Besides, how could I explain?

"But Catty, with you there I'd be thinking of you instead of the problem."

"Ah, Hodge, have we already been married so long you must get away from me to think?"

"No matter how long, that time will never come. Perhaps I'm wrong, Catty. It's just a feeling I have."

Her look was tragic with understanding. "You must do as you think right. Don't . . . don't be gone too long, my dear."

I dressed in clothes I often used for walking trips, clothes which bore no mark of any fashion and might pass as current wear among the poorer classes in any era of the past hundred years. I put a packet of dried beef in my pocket and started for the workshop.

As soon as I left the cottage I laughed at my hypersensitivity, at all the to-do I'd made over lying to Catty. This was but the first excursion; I planned others for the months after Gettysburg. There was no reason why she shouldnt accompany me on them. I grew lighthearted as my conscience eased and I even congratulated myself on my skill in not having told a single technical falsehood to Catty. I began to whistle, never a habit of mine, as I made my way along the path to the workshop.

Barbara was alone. Her ginger hair gleamed in the light of a gas globe; her eyes were green as they always were when she was exultant. "Well, Hodge?"

"Well, Barbara, I . . ."

"Have you told Catty?"

"Not exactly. How did you know?"

"I knew before you did, Hodge. After all, we're not strangers. All right. How long do you want to stay?"

"Four days."

"That's long for a first trip. Don't you think you'd better try a few sample minutes?"

"Why? Ive seen you and Ace go often enough and heard your accounts. I'll take care of myself. Have you got it down fine enough yet so you can invariably pick the hour of arrival?"

"Hour and minute," she answered confidently. "What'll it be?"

"About midnight of June 30, 1863," I answered. "I want to come back on the night of July Fourth."

"Youll have to be more exact than that. For the return, I mean. The dials are set on seconds."

"All right, make it midnight going and coming then."

"Have you a watch that keeps perfect time?"

"I don't know about perfect—"

"Take this one. It's synchronized with the master control clock." She handed me a large, rather awkward timepiece which had two independent faces side by side. "We had a couple made like this; the duplicate dials were useful before we were able to control HX-1 so exactly. One shows 1952 Haggershaven time."

"Ten thirty-three and fourteen seconds," I said.

"Yes. The other will show 1863 time. You won't be able to reset the first dial—but for goodness sake remember to keep it wound—and set the second for . . . 11:54, zero. That means in six minutes youll leave, to arrive at midnight. Remember to keep that one wound too, for youll go by that regardless of variations in local clocks. Whatever else happens, be in the center of the barn at midnight —allow yourself some leeway—by midnight, July Fourth. I don't want to have to go wandering around 1863 looking for you."

"You won't. I'll be here."

"Five minutes. Now then, food."

"I have some," I answered, slapping my pocket.

"Not enough. Take this concentrated chocolate along. I suppose it won't hurt to drink the water if youre not observed, but avoid their food. One never knows what chain might be started by the casual theft—or purchase, if you had enough old coins—of a loaf of bread. The possibilities are limitless and frightening. Listen: how can I impress on you the importance of doing nothing that could possibly change the future—our present? I'm sure to this day Ace doesnt understand, and I tremble every moment he spends in the past. The most trivial action may begin a series of disastrous consequences. Don't be seen, don't be heard. Make your trip as a ghost."

"Barbara, I promise I'll neither assassinate General Lee nor give the North the idea of a modern six-barreled cannon."

"Four minutes. It's not a joke, Hodge."

"Believe me," I said, "I understand."

She looked at me searchingly. Then she shook her head and began making her round of the engines, adjusting the dials. I slid under the glass ring as I'd so often seen her do and stood casually under the reflector. I was not in the least nervous. I don't think I was even particularly excited.

"Three minutes," said Barbara.

I patted my breast pocket. Notebook, pencils. I nodded.

She ducked under the ring and came toward me. "Hodge . . ."

"Yes?"

She put her arms on my shoulders, leaning forward. I kissed her, a little absently. "Clod!"

I looked at her closely, but there were none of the familiar signs of anger. "A minute to go, it says here," I told her.

She drew away and went back. "All set. Ready?"

"Ready," I answered cheerfully. "See you midnight, July Fourth, 1863."

"Right. Goodbye, Hodge. Glad you didnt tell Catty."

The expression on her face was the strangest I'd ever seen her wear. I could not, then or now, quite interpret it. Doubt, malice, suffering, vindictiveness, entreaty, love, were all there as her hand moved the switch. I began to answer something—perhaps to bid her wait—then the light made me blink and I too experienced the shattering feeling of transition. My bones seemed to fly from each other; every cell in my body exploded to the ends of space.

The instant of translation was so brief it is hard to believe all the multitude of impressions occurred simultaneously. I was sure my veins were drained of blood, my brain and eyeballs dropped into a bottomless void, my thoughts pressed to the finest powder and blown a universe away. Most of all, I knew the awful sensation of being, for that tiny fragment of time, not Hodgins McCormick Backmaker, but part of an *I* in which the I that was me merged all identity.

Then I opened my eyes. I was emotionally shaken; my knees and wrists were watery points of helplessness, but I was alive and functioning, with my individuality unimpaired. The light had vanished. I was in darkness save for faint moonlight coming through the cracks in the barn. The sweetish smell of cattle was in my nostrils, and the slow, ponderous stamp of hooves in my ears. I had gone back through time.

19. GETTYSBURG

$\mathcal{T}$HE BARKING of the dogs was frenzied, filled with the hoarse note indicating they had been raising the alarm for a long time without being heeded. I knew they must have been baying at the alien smells of soldiers for the past day, so I was not apprehensive that their scent of me would bring investigation. How Barbara and Ace had escaped detection on journeys which didnt coincide with abnormal events was beyond me; with such an unnerving racket in prospect I would either have given up the trips or moved the apparatus.

Strange, I reflected, that the cows and horses were undisturbed. That no hysterical chicken leaped from the roost in panic. Only the dogs scented my unnatural presence. Dogs who, as Mr Haggerwells remarked, are supposed to sense things beyond the perceptions of man.

Warily I picked my way past the livestock and out of the barn, fervently hoping the dogs were tied, for I had no mind to start my adventure by being bitten. Barbara's warnings seemed inadequate indeed; one would think she or Ace might have devised some method of neutralizing the infernal barking. But of course they could hardly do so without violating her rule of non-interference.

Once out on the familiar Hanover road every petty feeling of doubt or disquiet fell away and all the latent excitement took hold of me. I was gloriously in 1863, half a day and some thirty miles from the battle of Gettysburg. If there is a paradise for historians I had achieved it without the annoyance of dying first. I swung along at a good pace, thankful I had trained myself for long tramps, so that thirty miles in less than ten hours was no monstrous feat. The noise of the dogs died away behind me and I breathed the night air joyfully.

I had already decided I dared not attempt to steal a ride on the railroad, even supposing the cars were going through. As I turned off the Hanover road and took the direct one to Gettysburg, I knew I would not be able to keep on it for any length of time. Part of Early's Confederate division was moving along it from recently occupied York; Stuart's cavalry was all around; trifling skirmishes were being fought on or near it; Union troops, regulars as well as the militia called out by Governor Curtin for the emergency, were behind and ahead of me, marching for the Monocacy and Cemetery Ridge.

Leaving the highway would hardly slow me down, for I knew every sideroad, lane, path or shortcut, not only as they existed in my day, but as they had been in the time where I was now. I was going to need this knowledge even more on my return, for on the Fourth of July this road, like every other, would be glutted with beaten Northern troops, supplies and wounded left behind, frantically trying to reorganize as they were harassed by Stuart's cavalry and pressed by the victorious men of Hill, Longstreet, and Ewell. It was with this in mind I had allowed disproportionately longer for coming back.

I saw my first soldier a few miles further on, a jagged shadow sitting by the roadside with his boots off, massaging his feet. I guessed him Northern from his kepi, but this was not conclusive, for many Southron regiments wore kepis also. I struck off quietly into the field and skirted around him. He never looked up.

At dawn I estimated I was halfway, and except for the sight of that single soldier I might have been taking a nocturnal stroll through a countryside at peace. I was tired but certainly not worn out, and I knew I could count on nervous energy and happy excitement to keep me going long after my muscles began to protest. Progress would be slower from now on—Confederate infantry must be just ahead—even so, I should be at Gettysburg by six or seven.

The sudden drumming of hooves brushed me off the dusty pike and petrified me into rigidity as a troop dressed in gray and dirty tan galloped by screaming, "Eeeeee-yeeee" exultantly. The gritty cloud they stirred up settled slowly; I felt the particles sting my face and eyes. It would be the sideroads from now on, I determined.

Others had the same impulse; the sideroads were well populated. Although I knew the movement of every division and of many regiments, and even had some considerable idea of the civilian dislocation, the picture around me was jumbled and turbulent. Farmers, merchants, workers in overalls rode or tramped eastward; others, identical in dress and obvious intensity of effort, pushed westward. I passed carriages and carts with women and children traveling at various speeds both ways. Squads and companies of blue-clad troops marched along the roads or through the fields, trampling the crops, a confused sound of singing, swearing, or aimless talk hanging above them like a fog. Spaced by pacific intervals, men in gray or butternut, otherwise indistinguishable, marched in the same direction. I decided I could pass unnoticed in the milling crowds.

It is not easy for the historian, ten, fifty or five hundred years away from an event, to put aside for a moment the large concepts of currents and forces, or the mechanical aids of statistics, charts, maps, neat plans and diagrams in which the migration of men, women and children is indicated by an arrow, or a brigade of half-terrified, half-heroic men becomes a neat little rectangle. It is not easy to see behind source material, to visualize state papers, reports, letters, diaries as written by men who spent most of their lives sleeping, eating, yawning, eliminating, squeezing blackheads, lusting, looking out of windows, or talking about nothing in general with no one in particular. We are too impressed with the pattern revealed to us—or which we think has been revealed to us—to remember that for the participants history is a haphazard affair, apparently aimless, produced by human beings whose concern is essentially with the trivial and irrelevant. The historian is always conscious of destiny. The participants rarely—or mistakenly.

So to be set down in the midst of crisis, to be at once involved and apart, is to experience a constant series of shocks against which there is no anesthetic. The soldiers, the stragglers, the refugees, the farm boys shouting at horses, the tophatted gentlemen cursing the teamsters, the teamsters cursing back; the looters, pimps, gamblers, whores, nurses and newspapermen were indisputably what they appeared: vitally important to themselves, of little interest to anyone else. Yet at the same time they were a paragraph, a page, a chapter, a whole series of volumes.

I'm sure I was faithful to the spirit if not the letter of Barbara's warnings, and that none of the hundreds whom I passed or who passed me noted my presence, except cursorily. I, on the other hand, had to repress the constant temptation to peer into every face for signs which could not tell me what fortune or misfortune the decision of the next three days would bring to it.

A few miles from town the crowded disorder became even worse, for the scouts from Ewell's Corps, guarding the Confederate left flank on the York Road, acted like a cork in a bottle. Because I, unlike the other travelers, knew this, I cut sharply south to get back on the circuitous Hanover road I had left shortly after midnight, and crossing the bridge over Rock Creek, stumbled into Gettysburg.

The two and a half storey brick houses with their purplish slate roofs were placid and charming in the hot July sun. A valiant rooster pecked at horsedung in the middle of the street, heedless of the swarming soldiers, any of whom might take a notion for roast chicken. Privates in the black hats of the Army of the Potomac, cavalrymen with wide yellow stripes and cannoneers with red ones on the seams of their pants, swaggered importantly. Lieutenants with hands resting gracefully on sword hilts, captains with arms thrust in unbuttoned tunics, colonels smoking cigars, all moved back and forth across the street, out of and into houses and stores, each clearly intent on some business which would affect the course of the war. Now and then a general rode his horse through the crowd, slowly and thoughtfully, oppressed by the cares of rank. Soldiers spat, leered at an occasional woman, sat dolefully on handy stoops, or marched smartly toward an unknown destination. On the courthouse staff the flag hung doubtfully in the limp summer air. Every so often there was a noise like poorly organized thunder.

Imitating the adaptable infantrymen, I found an unoccupied stoop and sat down after a curious glance at the house, wondering whether it contained someone whose letters or diaries I had read. Drawing out my packet of dried beef, I munched away without taking any of my attention from the sights and sounds and smells around me. Only I knew how desperately these soldiers would fight this afternoon and all day tomorrow. I alone knew how they would be caught in the inescapable trap on July Third and finally routed, to begin the last act of the war. That major, I thought, so proud of his new-won golden oak leaves, may have an arm or leg shot off vainly defending Culp's Hill; that sergeant over there may lie faceless under an apple tree before nightfall.

Soon these men would be swept away from the illusory shelter of the houses and out onto the ridges where they would be pounded into defeat and disaster. There was nothing for me now in Gettysburg itself, though I could have spent days absorbing the color and feeling. Already I had tempted fate by my casual appearance in the heart of town. At any moment someone might speak to me, to ask for a light or a direction; an ill-considered word or action of mine might change, with ever-widening consequences, the course of the future. I had been foolish enough long enough; it was time for me to go to the vantage point I had decided upon and observe without peril of being observed.

I rose and stretched, my bones protesting. But a couple of miles more would see me clear of all danger of chance encounter with a too friendly or inquisitive soldier or civilian. I gave a last look, trying to impress every detail on my memory, and turned south on the Emmitsburg Road.

This was no haphazard choice. I knew where and when the crucial, the decisive move upon which all the other moves depended would take place. While thousands of men were struggling and dying on other parts of the battleground, a Confederate advance force, unnoticed, disregarded, would occupy the position which would eventually dominate the scene and win the battle—and the war—for the South. Heavy with knowledge no one else possessed I made my way toward a farm on which there was a wheatfield and a peach orchard.

20. BRING THE JUBILEE

$\mathcal{A}$ GREAT BATTLE in its first stages is as tentative, uncertain, and indefinite as a courtship just begun. At the beginning the ground was there for either side to take without protest; the other felt no surge of possessive jealousy. I walked unscathed along the Emmitsburg Road; on my left I knew there were Union forces concealed, on my right the Southrons maneuvered. In a few hours, to walk between the lines would mean instant death, but now the declaration had not been made, the vows had not been finally exchanged. It was still possible for either party to withdraw; no furious heat bound the two indissolubly together. I heard the periodic shell and the whine of a minie bullet; mere flirtatious gestures so far.

Despite the hot sun the grass was cool and lush. The shade in the orchard was velvety. From a low branch I picked a near ripe peach and sucked the wry juice. I sprawled on the earth and waited. For miles around, men from Maine and Wisconsin, from Georgia and North Carolina, assumed the same attitude. But I knew for what I was waiting; they could only guess.

Some acoustical freak dimmed the noises in the air to little more than amplification of the normal summer sounds. Did the ground really tremble faintly, or was I translating my mental picture of the marching armies, the great wagon trains, the heavy cannon, the iron-shod horses into an imagined physical effect? I don't think I dozed, but certainly my attention withdrew from the rows of trees with their scarred and runneled bark, curving branches and

181

graceful leaves, so that I was taken unaware by the unmistakable clump and creak of mounted men.

The blue-uniformed cavalry rode slowly through the peach orchard. They seemed like a group of aimless hunters returning from the futile pursuit of a fox; they chatted, shouted at each other, walked their horses abstractedly. One or two had their sabres out; they rose in their saddles and cut at the branches overhead in pure, pointless mischief.

Behind them came the infantrymen, sweating and swearing, more serious. Some few had wounds, others were without their muskets. Their dark blue tunics were carelessly unbuttoned, their lighter pants were stained with mud and dust and grass. They trampled and thrashed around like men long weary. Quarrels rose among them swiftly and swiftly petered out. No one could mistake them for anything but troops in retreat.

After they had passed, the orchard was still again, but the stillness had a different quality from what had gone before. The leaves did not rustle, no birds chirped, there were no faint betrayals of the presence of chipmunks or squirrels. Only if one listened very closely was the dry noise of insects perceptible. But I heard the guns now. Clearly and louder. And more continuously—much more continuously. It was not yet the full roar of battle, but death was authentic in its low rumble.

Then the Confederates came. Cautiously, but not so cautiously that one could fail to recognize they represented a victorious, invading army. Shabby they certainly were, as they pushed into the orchard, but alert and confident. Only a minority had uniforms which resembled those prescribed by regulation and these were torn, grimy and scuffed. Many of the others wore the semiofficial butternut—crudely dyed homespun, streaked and muddy brown. Some had ordinary clothes with military hats and buttons; a few were dressed in federal blue trousers with gray or butternut jackets.

Nor were their weapons uniform. There were long rifles, short carbines, muskets of varying age, and I noticed one bearded soldier with a ponderous shotgun. But whatever their dress or arms, their bearing was the bearing of conquerors. If I alone on the field that day knew for sure the outcome of the battle, these Confederate soldiers were close behind in sensing the future.

The straggling Northerners had passed me by with the clouded perception of the retreating. These Southrons, however, were steadfastly attentive to every sight and sound. Too late I realized the difficulty of remaining unnoticed by such sharp, experienced eyes. Even as I berated myself for my stupidity, a great, whiskery fellow in what must once have been a stylish bottle-green coat pointed his gun at me.

"Yank here boys!" Then to me, "What you doing here, fella?"

Three or four came up and surrounded me curiously. "Funniest lookin damyank I ever did see. Looks like he just fell out of a bathtub."

Since I had walked all night on dusty roads I could only think their standards of cleanliness were not high. And indeed this was confirmed by the smell coming from them: the stink of sweat, of clothes long slept in, of unwashed feet and stale tobacco.

"I'm a noncombatant," I said foolishly.

"Whazzat?" asked the beard. "Some kind of Baptist?"

"Naw," corrected one of the others. "It's a law-word. Means not all right in the head."

"Looks all right in the foot though. Let's see your boots, Yank. Mine's sure wore out."

What terrified me now was not the thought of my boots being stolen, or of being treated as a prisoner, or even the remote chance of being shot as a spy. A greater, more indefinite catastrophe was threatened by my exposure. These men were the advance company of a regiment due to sweep through the orchard and the wheatfield, explore that bit of wild ground known as the Devil's Den and climb up Little Round Top closely followed by an entire Confederate brigade. This was the brigade which held the Round Top for several hours until artillery was brought up, artillery which dominated the entire field and gave the South victory at Gettysburg.

There was no allowance for a pause, no matter how trifling, in the peach orchard, in any of the accounts I'd read or heard of. The hazard Barbara had warned so insistently against had happened. I had been discovered, and the mere discovery had altered the course of history.

I tried to shrug it off. Delay of a few minutes could hardly make a significant difference. All historians agreed that the capture of the Round Tops was an inevitability; the Confederates would have been foolish to overlook them—in fact it was hardly possible they could, prominent as they were both on maps and in physical reality—and they had occupied them hours before the Federals made a belated attempt to take them. I had been unbelievably stupid to expose myself, but I had created no repercussions likely to spread beyond the next few minutes.

"Said let's see them boots. Aint got all day to wait."

A tall officer with a pointed imperial and a sandy, faintly reddish mustache whose curling ends shone waxily came up, revolver in hand. "What's going on here?"

"Just a Yank, Capn. Making a little change of footgear." The tone was surly, almost insolent.

The galloons on the officer's sleeve told me the title was not honorary. "I'm a civilian, Captain," I protested. "I realize I have no business here."

The captain looked at me coldly, with an expression of disdainful contempt. "Local man?" he asked.

"Not exactly. I'm from York."

"Too bad. Thought you could tell me about the Yanks up ahead. Jenks, leave the civilian gentleman in full possession of his boots."

There was rage behind that sneer, a hateful anger apparently directed at me for being a civilian, at his men for their obvious lack of respect, at the battle, the world. I suddenly realized his face was intimately familiar. Irritatingly, because I could connect it with no name, place or circumstance.

"How long have you been in this orchard, Mister Civilian-From-York?"

The effort to identify him nagged me, working in the

depths of my mind, obtruding even into that top layer which was concerned with what was going on.

What was going on? *Too bad. Thought you could tell me about the Yanks up ahead. How long have you been in this orchard?*

Yanks up ahead? There werent any. There wouldnt be, for hours.

"I said, 'How long you been in this orchard?' "

Probably an officer later promoted to rank prominent enough to have his picture in one of the minor narratives. Yet I was certain his face was no likeness I'd seen once in a steel engraving and dismissed. These were features often encountered . . .

"Sure like to have them boots. If we aint fightin for Yankee boots, what the hell we fightin for?"

What could I say? That I'd been in the orchard for half an hour? The next question was bound to be, Had I seen Federal troops? Whichever way I answered I would be betraying my role of spectator.

"Hey Capn—this fella knows something. Lookit the silly grin!"

Was I smiling? In what? Terror? Perplexity? In the mere effort of keeping silent, so as to be involved no further?

"Tell yah—he's laughin cuz he knows somethin!"

Let them hang me, let them strip me of my boots; from here on I was dumb as dear Catty had been once.

"Out with it man—youre in a tight spot. Are there Yanks up ahead?"

The confusion in my mind approached chaos. If I knew the captain's eventual rank I could place him. Colonel Soandso. Brigadier-General Blank. What had happened? Why had I let myself be discovered? Why had I spoken at all and made silence so hard now?

"Yanks up ahead—they's Yanks up ahead!"

"Quiet you! I asked him—he didnt say there were Yanks ahead."

"Hay! Damyanks up above. Goin to mow us down!"

"Fella says the bluebellies are layin fur us!"

Had the lie been in my mind, to be telepathically plucked

by the excited soldiers? Was even silence no refuge from participation?

"Man here spotted the whole Fed artillery up above, trained on us!"

"Pull back, boys! Pull back!"

I'd read often enough of the epidemic quality of a perfectly unreasonable notion. A misunderstood word, a baseless rumor, an impossible report, was often enough to set a group of armed men—squad or army—into senseless mob action. Sometimes the infection made for feats of heroism, sometimes for panic. This was certainly less than panic, but my nervous, meaningless smile conveyed a message I had never sent.

"It's a trap. Pull back boys—let's get away from these trees and out where we can see the Yanks!"

The captain whirled on his men. "Here, damn you," he shouted furiously, "you all gone crazy? The man said nothing. There's no trap!"

The men moved slowly, sullenly away. "I heard him," one of them muttered, looking accusingly toward me.

The captain's shout became a yell. "Come back here! Back here, I say!"

His raging stride overtook the still irresolute men. He grabbed the one called Jenks by the shoulder and whirled him about. Jenks tried to jerk free. There was fear on his face, and hate. "Leave me go, damn you," he screamed, "Leave me go!"

The captain yelled at his men again. Jenks snatched at the pistol with his left hand; the officer pulled the gun away. Jenks brought his musket upright against the captain's body, the muzzle just under his chin, and pushed—as though the firearm somehow gave him leverage. They wrestled briefly, then the musket went off.

The captain's hat flew upward, and for an instant he stood, bareheaded, in the private's embrace. Then he fell. Jenks wrenched his musket free and disappeared.

When I came out of my shock I walked over to the body. The face had been blown off. Shreds of human meat dribbled bloodily on the gray collar and soiled the fashionably long hair. I had killed a man. Through my interference with the past I had killed a man who had been destined to longer life and even some measure of fame. I was the guilty sorcerer's apprentice.

I stooped down to put my hands inside his coat for papers which would tell me who he was and satisfy the curiosity which still basely persisted. It was not shame which stopped me. Just nausea, and remorse.

I saw the Battle of Gettysburg. I saw it with all the unique advantages of a professional historian thoroughly conversant with the patterns, the movements, the details, who knows where to look for the coming dramatic moment, the recorded decisive stroke. I fulfilled the chroniclers' dream.

It was a nightmare.

To begin with, I slept. I slept not far from the captain's body in the peach orchard. This was not callousness, but physical and emotional exhaustion. When I went to sleep the guns were thundering; when I woke they were thundering louder. It was late afternoon. I thought immediately, this is the time for the futile Union charge against the Round Tops.

But the guns were not sounding from there. All the roar was northward, from the town. I knew how the battle went; I had studied it for years. Only now it wasnt happening the way it was written down in the books.

True, the first day was a Confederate victory. But it was not the victory we knew. It was just a little different, just a little short of the triumph recorded. And on the second day, instead of the Confederates getting astride the Taney-town Road and into the position from which they tore Meade's army to bits from three sides, I witnessed a terrible encounter in the peach orchard and the wheatfield—places known to be safely behind the Southron lines.

All my life I'd heard of Pickett's charge on the third day. Of how the disorganized Federals were given the final killing blow in their vitals. Well, I saw Pickett's charge on the third day and it was not the same charge in the historic place. It was a futile attempt to storm superior positions

(positions, by established fact, in Lee's hands since July First) ending in slaughter and defeat.

Defeat for the South, not the North. Meade's army was not broken; the Confederates could not scatter and pursue them now. The Capitulation, if it ever took place, would come under different circumstances. The independence of the Confederate States might not be acknowledged for years. If at all.

All because the North held the Round Tops.

Years more of killing, and possibly further years of guerrilla warfare. Thousands and thousands of dead, their blood on my hands. A poisoned continent, an inheritance of hate. Because of me.

I cannot tell you how I got back to York. If I walked, it was somnambulistically. Possibly I rode the railroad or in a farmer's cart. Part of my mind, a tiny part that kept coming back to pierce me no matter how often I crushed it out, remembered those who died, those who would have lived, but for me. Another part was concerned only with the longing to get back to my own time, to the haven, to Catty. A much larger part was simply blank, except for the awesome, incredible knowledge that the past could be changed—that the past *had* been changed.

I must have wound my watch—Barbara's watch—for it was ten oclock on the night of July Fourth when I got to the barn. Ten oclock by 1863 time; the other dial showed it to be 8:40, that would be twenty of nine in the morning, 1952 time. In two hours I would be home, safe from the nightmare of happenings that never happened, of guilt for the deaths of men not supposed to die, of the awful responsibility of playing destiny. If I could not persuade Barbara to smash her damnable contrivance I would do so myself.

The dogs barked madly, but I was sure no one heeded. It was the Fourth of July, and a day of victory and rejoicing for all Pennsylvanians. I stole into the barn and settled myself in the exact center, even daring the use of a match, my last one, to be sure I'd be directly under the reflector when it materialized.

I could not sleep, though I longed to blot out the horror and wake in my own time. Detail by detail I went over what I had seen, superimposing it like a palimpsest upon the history I'd always known. Sleep would have kept me from this wretched compulsion and from questioning my sanity, but I could not sleep.

I have heard that in moments of overwhelming shock some irrelevancy, some inconsequential matter persistently forces itself on the attention. The criminal facing execution thinks, not of his imminent fate or of his crime, but of the cigarette stub he left burning in his cell. The bereaved widow dwells, not on her lost husband, but on tomorrow's laundry. So it was with me. Behind that part of my mind re-living the past three days, a more elementary part gnawed at the identification of the slain captain.

I knew that face. Particularly did I know that face set in a sneer, distorted with anger. But I could not remember it in Confederate uniform. I could not remember it with sandy mustaches. And yet the sandy, reddish hair, revealed in that terrible moment when his hat flew off, was as familiar as part of the face. Oh, I thought, if I could only place it once and for all and free my mind at least of this trivial thing.

I wished there were some way I could have seen the watch, to concentrate on the creeping progress of the hands and distract myself from the wave after wave of wretched meditations which flowed over me. But the moonlight was not strong enough to make the face distinguishable, much less the figures on the dials. There was no narcotic.

As one always is at such times I was convinced the appointed moment had passed unnoticed. Something had gone wrong. Over and over I had to tell myself that minutes seem hours in the waiting dark; it might feel like two or three in the morning to me; it was probably barely eleven. No use. A minute—or an hour or a second—later I was again positive midnight had passed.

Finally I began to suffer a monstrous illusion. I began to think it was getting lighter. That dawn was coming. Of course I knew it could not be; what I fancied lifting darkness was only a sick condition of swollen, overtired eyes. Dawn does not come to Pennsylvania at midnight, and it was not yet midnight. At midnight I would be back at Haggershaven, in 1952.

Even when the barn was fully lighted by the rising sun and I could see the cattle peaceful in their stalls I refused to believe what I saw. I took out my watch only to find something had disturbed the works; the hands registered five oclock. Even when the farmer, milk pails over arm, started in surprise, exclaiming, "Hay, what you doing here?"—even then, I did not believe.

Only when, as I opened my mouth to explain to my involuntary host, did something happen. The puzzle which had pursued me for three days suddenly solved itself. I knew why the face of the Southron captain had been so familiar. Familiar beyond any of the better known warriors on either side. I had indeed known that face intimately; seen those features enraged or sneering. The nose, the mouth, the eyes, the expression were Barbara Haggerwells'. The man dead in the peach orchard was the man whose portrait hung in the library of Haggershaven, its founder, Herbert Haggerwells. Captain Haggerwells— never to become a major now, or buy this farm. Never to marry a local girl or beget Barbara's great grandfather. Haggershaven had ceased to exist in the future.

21. FOR THE TIME BEING

I AM WRITING this, as I said, in 1877. I am a healthy man of forty-five, no doubt with many years ahead of me. I might live to be a hundred, except for an illogical feeling that I must die before 1921. However, eighty-nine should be enough for anyone. So I have ample time to put my story down. Still, better to have it down and done with; should anything happen to me tomorrow it will be on paper.

For what? As confession and apology? As an inverted substitute for the merciful amnesia which ought to have erased my memory as well as my biography? (I have written to Wappinger Falls; there are no records of any Hodgins family, or of Backmakers. Does this mean the forces I set in motion destroyed Private Hodgins as well as Captain Haggerwells? Or only that the Hodginses and Backmakers settled elsewhere? In either case I am like Adam— in this world—a special, parentless creation.) There is no one close enough to care, or intimate enough to accept my word in the face of all reason. I have not married in this time, nor shall I. I write only as old men talk to themselves.

The rest of my personal story is simple. The name of the farmer who found me in his barn was Thammis; they had need of a hired hand and I stayed on. I had no desire to go elsewhere; in fact I could not bear to leave what was—and will never be—Haggershaven.

In the beginning I used to go to the location of the Agati's garden and look across at the spot where I left our cottage and Catty. It was an empty pilgrimage. Now I content myself with the work which needs doing. I shall stay here till I die.

Catty. Haggershaven. Are they really gone, irrevocably lost, in a future which never existed, which couldnt exist, once the chain of causation was broken? Or do they exist after all, in a universe in which the South won the battle of Gettysburg and Major Haggerwells founded Haggershaven? Could another Barbara devise a means to reach that universe? I would give so much to believe this, but I cannot. I simply cannot.

Children know about such things. They close their eyes and pray, "Please God, make it didnt happen." Often they open their eyes to find it happened anyway, but this does not shake their faith that many times the prayer is granted. Adults smile, but can any of them be sure the memories they cherish were the same yesterday? Do they *know* that a past cannot be expunged? Children know it can.

And once lost, that particular past can never be regained. Another and another perhaps, but never the same one. There are no parallel universes—though this one may be sinuous and inconstant.

That this world is a better place than the one into which I was born, and promises to grow still better, seems true. What idealism lay behind the Southron cause triumphed in the reconciliation of men like Lee; what was brutal never got the upper hand as it did in my world. The Negro is free; black legislatures pass advanced laws in South Carolina; black congressmen comport themselves with dignity in Washington. The Pacific railroad is built, immigrants pour in to a welcoming country to make it strong and wealthy; no one suggests they should be shut out or hindered.

There are rumors of a deal between northern Republicans and southern Democrats, betraying the victory of the Civil War—how strange it is still, after fourteen years, to use this term instead of the familiar War of Southron Independence—in return for the presidency. If this is true, my brave new world is not so brave.

It may not be so new either. Prussia has beaten France and proclaimed a German Empire; is this the start in a different way of the German Union? Will 1914 see an Emperors' War—there is none in France now—leaving Germany facing . . . whom?

Any one of the inventions of my own time would make me a rich man if I could reproduce them, or cared for money. With mounting steel production and the tremendous jump in population, what a success the minible would be. Or the tinugraph. Or controllable balloons.

The typewriter I have seen. It has developed along different and clumsier lines; inevitably, I suppose, given initial divergence. It may mean greater advances; more likely not. The universal use of gaslight must be far in the future if it is to come at all; certainly its advent is delayed by all this talk of inventing electric illumination. If we couldnt put electricity to work it's unlikely my new contemporaries will be able to. Why, they havent even made the telegraph cheap and convenient.

And something like HX-1? It is inconceivable. Could it be that in destroying the future in which Haggershaven existed I have also destroyed the only dimension in which time travel was possible?

So strangely easily I can write the words, "I destroyed." Catty.

But what of Tyss's philosophy? Is it possible I shall be condemned to repeat the destruction throughout eternity? Have I written these lines an infinite number of times before? Or is the mercy envisaged by Enfandin a reality? And what of Barbara's expression as she bade me goodbye? Could she possibly

Editorial note by Frederick Winter Thammis: Quite recently, in the summer of 1953 to be exact, I commissioned the remodelling of my family home near York, Pennsylvania. Among the bundles of old books and papers stored in the attic was a box of personal effects, labelled "H M Backmaker." In it was the manuscript concluding with an unfinished sentence, reproduced above.

My father used to tell me that when he was a boy there was an old man living on the farm, nominally as a hired hand, but actually as a pensioner, since he was beyond the age of useful labor. My father said the children considered him not quite right in his mind, but very entertaining, for he often repeated long, disjointed narratives of an impossible world and an impossible society which they found as fascinating as the Oz books. On looking back, he said, Old Hodge talked like an educated man, but this might simply be the impression of young, uncultivated minds.

Clearly it was in some attempt to give form and unity to his tales that the old man wrote his fable down, and then was too shy to submit it for publication. This is the only reasonable way to account for its existence. Of course he says he wrote it in 1877, when he was far from old, and disconcertingly, analysis of the paper shows it might have been written then.

Two other items should be noted. In the box of Backmaker's belongings there was a watch of unknown manufacture and unique design. Housed in a cheap nickel case, the jeweled movement is of extraordinary precision and delicacy. The face has two dials, independently set and wound.

The second is a quotation. It can be matched by similar quotations in any of half a hundred volumes on the Civil War. I pick this only because it is handy. From W. E. Woodward's *Years of Madness*, p. 202:

". . . Union troops that night and next morning took a position on Cemetery Hill and Round Top . . . The Confederates could have occupied this position but they failed to do so. It was an error with momentous consequences."

Ward Moore was born in New Jersey in 1903. Well known for his work outside the SF field, his debut novel was the picaresque *Breath the Air Again*. His first SF novel was the comic *Greener Than You Think* (1947), which was followed six years later by *Bring the Jubilee* (1953). He died in 1978.

SF MASTERWORKS

*'An amazing list – genuinely the best novels
from sixty years of SF'* – Iain M. Banks

ONE BOOK WILL BE PUBLISHED PER MONTH.
THE FIRST 6 MONTHS OF THE 2001 PROGRAMME
ARE AS FOLLOWS:

#37 NOVA Samuel R. Delany
'The best science fiction writer in the world' Algis Budrys

#38 THE FIRST MEN IN THE MOON
H. G. Wells
'Wells' scientific romances were works of art'
Arthur C. Clarke

#39 THE CITY AND THE STARS
Arthur C. Clarke
*'One of the most imaginative novels of the
far future ever written'* Sunday Times

#40 BLOOD MUSIC Greg Bear
'Classic science fiction' New Scientist

#41 JEM Frederik Pohl
*'The most consistently able writer science fiction
has yet produced'* Kingsley Amis

#42 BRING THE JUBILEE Ward Moore
'A classic alternative world story'
Brian Aldiss

SF MASTERWORKS